365 DAYS OF A SUFI

365 DAYS OF A SUFI
A Journal of Love, Dreams & Freedom

SONIA MACKWANI

Leadstart

ISBN: 978-93-5559-075-6
© Sonia Mackwani, 2022
Cover design: Harshad Marathe
Printing: Printone Graphics Mumbai

Published in India 2022 by
Leadstart
A Division of One Point Six Technologies Pvt Ltd
Building J2, Shram Seva Premises, Offices: 119-123
Wadala Truck Terminus, Wadala (East)
Mumbai 400 037, Maharashtra, INDIA
T + 91 96 99933000   **E** info@leadstartcorp.com
W www.leadstartcorp.com

What after enlightenment?

What after the end of a journey?

What after achieving love, freedom and dream? All of it!

What next?

ABOUT THE AUTHOR

Multiple award-winner *Sonia Mackwani* is a Psychic Healer and Intuitive Channel. She has a Masters in Clinical Psychology and Hypnotherapy. An Author, she writes for both children and adults. She founded the non-profit organisation *Touching Lives,* which serves children and slum communities in Mumbai, through learning, healing and art-expression. A percentage of royalty from her works goes to this initiative. A screen-writing consultant, independent film-maker, and performing artist, she is also a trainer. She developed the *Self-Work* Approach Model* to coach companies/individuals in holistic wellness. She has worked extensively in both rural and urban sectors in support of learning and healing aids. She is also a channel for the *Master Reconnection Process*, aimed at creating our 8th sense, and a *Birth Into Being* facilitator, focussed on healing birth imprints and redesigning lives. She lives between India and Switzerland.

BOOKS, MUSIC, FILMS

Everyone Can Heal
The Rocket Science Called Love
Tales from Indian Mythology
Power Minutes – Meditation Audios, Times Music
Space, a short film

CONTACT
Facebook:https://www.facebook.com/touchinglives.
beingyou
Instagram:https://www.instagram.com/sonia_mackwani/
Twitter: https://twitter.com/TouchingLives
Website: https://www.touchonelife.org
www.soniamackwani.com

Imagine you are looking for something, and you find something else, that changes your world. *365 Days of a Sufi* was one such phenomenon for me. It strengthened my belief in the invisible forces of nature and in the precious gift we humans all have – intuition. In 2017, I had just completed a fiction book and thought to take a break from stories and write something in the non-fiction genre.

One of my practices is to design a book cover before I begin my work, so that I can bring the energy of that book into the creative-reality space. As I was looking at designs, I stumbled upon a starkly simple picture – palms folded in prayer, holding a *tasbih* (rosary). I was so inspired by this holy image that I immediately opened a Word file and began to channel the characters, especially Meru, the girl who finds freedom amidst her closed life.

Even as I connected with her for the first time in my imagination and creation, I could feel my heart, soul and mind going deep into meditative spaces en route to spiritual questions and answers. Thus, *365 Days Of A Sufi* came to me. I wrote it in 21 days, working for 21 minutes every morning, from 7:00am to 7:21am. This is my second practice in writing – giving it a timeline and devoting specific time. Every book speaks to me when it is the best time to channel it.

Without knowing where the story would lead next, where the characters would take me, which new ones were waiting for me to awaken and invest them with life, I would just show up on my computer religiously. On the 21ˢᵗ day, as channelled, *365 Days of a Sufi* was born. My third practice: not to chase, think, look for characters and stories except at the allotted time. It was like 7:00am to 7:21am was my visiting time, and post that, my normal life went on.

All the characters, names and places are fictitious. They have no link to any places, people, or incidents that may coincide with real ones. But, as much as the names are fictitious, their journeys and experiences are genuine, teaching us lessons for the real world; lessons about love, freedom and dreams. **Huma* - a mythical bird of Iranian legends and fables, and continuing as a common design in Sufi and Diwan poetry.

It was not till mid-2018, that I shared it with an editor-friend to work on, and in 2019, another editor-friend proofread it and helped me formulate an official proposal. The book had its own way of communicating with me towards its next step. In late 2019, that I sat to send it out to publishers, and began writing the non-fiction book I had earlier supposed I would write. When India went into complete lockdown in March 2020, when everything was getting sealed, when the whole world was in panic and fright, and all plans had been upended, I received a call from the coordinator at Leadstart, that they had accepted the work. That led me once again to believe in the serendipitous play of the universe. In those uncertain times, this came as a certain way forward.

The wait for the lockdown to lift was never-ending, so I decided to write yet another book, this time fiction. When I completed the work, I decided to launch a beta-readers process, and made an announcement on social media for volunteers to read my new book. Many people came forward. In one of those twists of fate, the book I felt impelled to send them to read was not my recent one, but *365 Days*

Of A Sufi. In a couple of weeks I received feedback – constructive, critical, creative and conscientious. It opened a window for me to look at the work differently. I re-edited the entire book and incorporated as much as I could from my editor and beta-readers' feedback and suggestions. It was a very interesting process. It gave me a new reason to reunite with the characters and stories once again.

I must not forget to mention that while half the world was still in lockdown even in early 2021, and India was about to hit the deadly second wave of the corona pandemic, I had an opportunity to fly to Switzerland. Amidst the snow and the mountains, the characters surrendered to being revised, redesigned, and edited. The book has travelled miles inside out. And I truly pray it opens pathways and windows for you to find your own essence of freedom. That it will ignite love in your soul once again and bring you the joy of realizing your wings, not just to fly alone, but to take along the world with you to dimensions that lead to evolution.

Early one morning, I learned that in Switzerland, if you lose your house-key, you have to make new keys for everyone living in the building. Why is that, you wonder? Because everyone uses the same key to open the main security door, and the same key to open the respective doors of their homes. Losing the key to your house can endanger the lives of others. Yet, with your house-key, you cannot open someone else's door. It is perhaps a smart lock system. It led me to think deeper, how everyone can have the same key but only you can access your own home. We all have to walk our own journeys. No one can walk on our behalf. If we walk, we lead the world, and if we don't, the world leads us.

This book thus comes as a key to access your own inner world.

Before I end, I would like to share that in summer the sun rises here in Switzerland at 5:31 a.m. and sets at 9:29pm. Long long days. When I sleep, the sun is still shining bright, the birds are chirping, and when I wake up, the birds trilling never seems to have stopped, nor the sun gone down. It is still in the sky, spreading its bright arms to the world. This gives me so much hope that time will heal all of us, and our beleaguered world. Nature will show us the way. And we shall overcome this pandemic to emerge as more humble, more compassionate and loving beings.

My love to you all.

PROLOGUE

Huma.

Her name!

Once upon a time, a mythical bird named *Huma* was born. She lived her entire life high up in the sky and never flew down to the earth. She laid her eggs amidst the puffy clouds too. Before the fragile eggs would strike the ground, the little ones inside would break through the shell with their beaks and take their first flight skyward, joining their radiant mother. Their fresh wings with those wonderful shining feathers looked effulgent and magical.

Huma was elegant and wise, and known for her unconditional love and generosity. It is said that whenever she flew over any human, the life of that soul became auspicious and blessings showered upon them, immortal and infinite. What a mystical legendary bird! For centuries it was known that those *Huma* had flown over, were the ones on the path of love, dreams and freedom.

And indeed, anyone who has begun their journey is always looking for one 'last' omen.

Huma happens to them, it is prayed.

PART I

CHAPTER 1

Meru looked around her house. It was just a small 10'x10' room, set amidst many other hutments, each attached to the next. The walls were lime green. A small arched window overlooked nothing beyond the grey and grim wall of another tatty house.

Her cot by the window was covered with a white threadbare bedsheet, the edges of which hung loose. She had scrubbed the floor several times and made sure that no cobwebs were homed in the corners. She had arranged all the vessels neatly on a small wooden rack. Her limited belongings including a tiny rusted *buksa*, her only treasure, kept inside the one *almirah* she had. Everything looked clean and orderly.

Casting a last glance over everything, she fixed her deep-set hazel eyes for a long moment on the framed picture of her parents, stuck on a cracked cardboard. She bowed, murmuring gently, *'Shukhar Alhamdulillah'*. Then she stepped out and locked the rotting wooden door behind her.

Pulling her scarf over her head, she picked up the little bag she had packed that morning. She was going to live with her only childhood friend, who came back after almost ten years. Her friend Zaitoon!

$$\mathcal{L}$$

CHAPTER 2

Meru grew up knowing only the world between the two forlorn streets where she lived, in the remote and rustic little town called Bashirbagh. She worked as a *zari* weaver in an old shop that sold scarves, shawls, kaftans and *keffiyehs*, the owner of which was an elderly man of old ways. Meru had called him Gulfam *Kaka* since the time she had barely learnt to utter a word and walk on her tiny feet. Gulfam *Kaka* would lift her up affectionately and play with her whenever she accompanied her *Abu,* who worked in the shop as a *zari* weaver.

'Meru is *rehemat. Niyamat,*' Gulfam *Kaka* believed, for after her birth, the shop had begun to pick up pace and receive orders not only from the Bashirbagh bazaar, but also from the neighbouring cities.

Later, when Meru's mother also started to lend a hand at hemming the increasing *zari* work, to fetch more money, Meru ate, played and slept in the shop as a matter of fact. Soon, weaving *zari* became her life too.

On her way to work every day, she would meet Esmail *Bhai* in the back alleys. He spent his days and nights fooling passers-by with his fake limb injuries, to fill his real stomach. Sometimes, he offered Meru food; he thought her adorable. He often sought blessings for Meru, praising her to all. Meru never judged Esmail *Bhai* for the way he chose to make a living. She missed him now, for his spot felt empty without his lies and ragged presence. A few weeks earlier, he had died of some undiagnosed but real illness.

Meru was docile and well-mannered, both at home and outside it. 'You have given her good *tameez*,' people would often tell her parents, who in their turn felt proud of the upbringing they had managed to impart despite their penury.

When her parents passed away in a tragic accident while returning from a neighbouring town where they had gone to pick up new stocks of threads and fabrics for the shop, Meru was left with nothing but freedom. She now lived alone, almost entirely free to live her life the way she wanted. She was answerable to no one, and had no one to question her. She was in her late teens but she had never been to school. Instead, she had been taught that work was everything. The habit of following her parents' instructions had taken root deep within her.

She was clueless whether she even had the right or ability to make her own decisions. She had no idea what freedom meant. She simply continued going to work, earning her daily wage, and living the same way she had always known.

Until one day, when Zaitoon showed up.

○

Zaitoon was her childhood friend. She had lived next door. Growing up, the two girls had built a loving bond and a strong friendship. But, when they were nine, Zaitoon had moved to a village far away, with her parents.

So when, after ten years, Zaitoon had suddenly appeared at the *zari* shop in Bashirbagh, both girls had rejoiced, their eyes welling with tears, their hearts filled to the brim with overwhelming love. It was as if a force of nature had brought them together again.

Zaitoon had grown into a beautiful young woman. Her eyes tantalising green, her lustrous hair tinged with *henna*, her gait feminine, her shoulders holding confidence and her face grit. Zaitoon held Meru's calloused palms, marvelling as she looked into her friend's sunken eyes, wanting to make sure it wasn't just a dream. It was not. Before her stood her childhood comrade Meru, who looked as thin as a rake. Her face was sallow and her skin, stretched taut over her cheekbones, her eyes stuck in time and innocence, her fingers bruised with marks of a thousand needle pricks and her lips, as thin as a *reshmi* thread.

Zaitoon jubilantly invited Meru to her late grandfather's house, to live with her for some time. She and her *Ammi* had recently migrated from their village to the neighbouring city of Otto, which was bigger, richer, more extravagant and modern compared to Bashirbagh. This was the first time Meru had finally stepped out of her little town for a holiday.

CHAPTER 3

Zaitoon lived with her mother in a more spacious house than Meru had ever been in, or even imagined. It was a large structure with high ceilings and wide rosewood-panelled windows, across which hung old stippled curtains under carved pelmets. It gave the place a palatial feel. Though archaic and rather bare, almost monastic, it looked like a palace to its new inhabitants. An antique wooden staircase with carved railings led to two bedrooms and a small storage room on the first floor. And to Meru's surprise, yet another staircase spiralled up to a vast terrace that, apart from overlooking the alluring and picturesque city of Otto, also gave a view onto an unkempt structure right on the opposite side of the street – a home for children; survivors of the war.

Zaitoon's grandfather's house, though ancient, was well looked after. The lean streets below were busy all day, filled with noisy cycle-rickshaws scuttling to and fro in a mad frenzy. And then there was this constant collective chatter of people from the alleyways.

Zaitoon made a living by tutoring young children in the house, teaching them whatever she knew of Math and Urdu. She had quit school early to help with the chores and look after her mother when Sakina had been left partially handicapped after her stroke. Sakina *Khala* was recovering better in the city than she had in the village, with good hakims and the change of atmosphere.

'She looks happier here,' Zaitoon told her friend.

Zaitoon and her *Ammi* had been astonished as Meru now was, when they had first arrived at the house. They couldn't believe fate had gifted them this unexpected inheritance. Sakina *Khala* had pulled herself together to do some basic cleaning and cooking, though she tired easily. Zaitoon would scold her affectionately and force her to lie down on the charpoy on the ground floor.

Sakina had not yet climbed the stairs to the rooms on the first floor. Most of her time was spent watching the world outside the window, as if fervently waiting for something or someone. Zaitoon often found her staring with puffy eyes at the frame hanging on a wainscoted wall in front of her. In the frame, stood an elegant and charming young man, perhaps of royal lineage, with multiple pearl necklaces garlanding his neck. A silk sash rested on one straight shoulder, and an imperial diamond-ruby crown sat on his head. Yet his eyes gleamed with subtle charm and he held a deferential composure. Perhaps he was a Prince or Sultan from the past. Neither Zaitoon nor her mother knew who he was, nor could they recollect any mention of such an elite personage. But, since Zaitoon's grandfather's *will* had specifically requested the painting not be taken down, the gilded frame with its enigmatic occupant remained where it had always hung.

○

That night, Zaitoon and Meru slept on the terrace beneath the sky, watching the stars, cosy under their warm blankets. They spoke of their childhood days and about all the things they had missed out on while apart. Most of the time it was Zaitoon who did the talking, while Meru listened to her friend intently.

'Do you think everything is perfect in your life?' Zaitoon asked Meru, whose gaze never seemed to shift from the shining Pole Star above them.

'What does that mean?'

'Perfect means…perfect!'

'I don't even know what imperfect means Zaitoon!'

Zaitoon looked at Meru, whose eyes were still glued to the star.

'I don't think you have changed since I left, all those years ago.'

Meru heaved a sigh and said, 'Neither have these stars, Zaitoon.'

Meru suddenly winced and turned to the other side. Tears trickled from the corner of her eyes. She couldn't handle the dose of freedom that was beginning to surface within her. She couldn't handle the realization that now her life was her own. Nobody owned it. She couldn't comprehend the infinite possibilities before her any more than she could decipher the vast heavens above her. The change of place, the open air, was overwhelming and frightening.

All she had ever known were those two streets in Bashirbagh; the surrounding back-alleys and that little home of hers. In that moment, her mind yearned for familiarity. The only sound she had ever heard were those of the neighbourhood children, who pranced in and around the puddles and garbage heaps all day long. She missed her thirteen-year-old neighbour Rahim, who had had one leg amputated, and spent his day silently watching the other children at play. She missed Gulfam *Kaka* and the bazaars of Bashirbagh. She couldn't fathom that there were other streets calling to her to walk upon, that there could be another home than what she had known; that there was one big sky under which there were many other bazaars, towns and cities.

Meru had never been more miserable than she felt at that moment. She was free to love anything, or anyone to whom she felt drawn. But both love and freedom scared her to death.

CHAPTER 4

It was midnight and Meru and Zaitoon were still catching up, silent and chatty in turn. Around them, the world had fallen asleep, grown cooler and quieter. Meru slid further under her blanket, her eyes still on those sequin-silver twinkling stars.

'Then, I remember Rahim, too. Is he still there?

'Hmm,' Meru responded.

'Truth to tell, I'm still scared of him, you know. How he would run after all the children to cut their hair with those scissors in his little hand. I cannot forget the staccato snipping sound of his scissors. As soon as he scooted out of his house, we'd run and hide behind some drum and throw stones at him to protect ourselves.'

Zaitoon sighed, lost in reflection. 'And then there you were one day, fearlessly standing in front of him and holding out a long lock of hair for him to cut! All the children were stunned, including Rahim, I think.' She chuckled, remembering his stunned face.

'Hmm...' Meru responded. 'He has mellowed since then and stopped harrowing all of us. I cannot believe he is an amputee now.'

Zaitoon sat bolt upright, her eyes wide. 'Is that true?' When Meru nodded silently, she lay back with a sigh. 'I think, it's a punishment, maybe!' Zaitoon pondered on that for a while and said, 'Anyway, now you ask me something. I have been doing all the talking.'

Meru paused for some time before she spoke. 'How far did you study in school, Zaitoon?'

'Till the 9th grade, in an Urdu medium school,' Zaitoon answered. 'But my *Abba* was familiar with the English language. So he would tutor me. Every night he would tell me the stories he had heard from his father. I've still got some of the original, handwritten ones!'

'You mean your grandfather's stories?'

'Yes, Meru.'

'Your grandfather was a writer?'

'I believe so. From what I have read so far. I've just begun to read them. I think he wrote more for himself. It was his personal thing. He wrote both in Urdu and in English. I remember spending time with him growing up, but then he went away somewhere to live alone. *Ammi* says he was an enlightened soul, who dedicated his life to practising *ibadat* and gaining *talim* till his final days. He wrote every day.'

'Was he a known writer?' Meru asked.

'All I know is that he was a shy person. Writing was important to him. I don't think, he was known. *Ammi* says that he wrote to help others walk the path of *sirat-al-mustakim.*'

'What is *sirat-al-mustakim*?' Meru asked innocently.

'It means the right path,' Zaitoon murmured.

'But why would someone who must have been already on the right path, want to read his book then?'

'Do you mean that you are on the right path?' Zaitoon quipped seriously.

'Zaitoon, I have no path!' Meru exclaimed.

In her mind, Meru went back to those familiar streets, her daily walk to the shop, the smells, the eateries and the walls – the only path she knew. She missed it all.

CHAPTER 5

It was the first morning Meru had ever awoken under the open sky. It was the first time her eyes had seen such vastness. The birds were chirping. The upper semi-circle of the sun was emerging on the horizon. It looked ageless, ever-radiant, glimmering between two tangerine mountains in the distance. There were puffy white clouds spread across the sky, here and there and the golden-silver linings gleamed around its undefined edges. The birds flocked together and disappeared far away somewhere.

It was an ethereal morning and Meru lingered on her makeshift mattress on the terrace, listening to the silence of this new dawn. The silence of that morning was quite unlike the familiar silence inside her. This morning she had nowhere to go. She did not have to clean the house, cook her food, run to work, weave *zari*, or do any of the things she had been doing relentlessly for years.

There was a small swing on the terrace that stood beside a few flowering potted plants. A serene breeze carried with it the fragrance of roses, lavender and lilies. She rose from her mattress, sat on the swing and gave an incredulous gasp! She saw that the clouds still held a faint blush in an unblemished moment of innocence. The town had yet to fully awaken to all its usual jostling and noise, though she could hear the first cries of vendors in the distance, eager to make the first sale of the day.

Across the street, she could see some movement in the Children's Home. She looked at the decrepit structure, the corroded walls, the tarnished windows, and the decapitated dome on the terrace, where several pigeons nested. Though the war was long over, the place still bore the wounds. It carried in its forlorn form some melancholic history.

Meru also noticed that the signage of the Home had not just lost its colour but its rusting corners had curled into jagged edges. It was hanging so loose that it could fall any second. She sensed that the entire place was in a terrible state.

Just then, she heard Zaitoon calling to her as she appeared on the terrace, carrying a tray. 'Oh good, you're awake!' she said.

Meru smiled at her energetic friend. The tray held a bowl of boiled green gram, garnished with some finely sliced coconut. There was also a bowl heaped high with dates, two cups of tea, and a hot snack.

Meru was astonished. It had been ages since she was served a grand breakfast with so much love. In Bashirbagh, it was only during *Ramadan* that *Abu* would bring home some *kunafehs*, or rice pudding, and sometimes *Ammi* would make *halva* on Friday evenings. Gulfam *Kaka* would give her *baksheesh*, which she would hoard like a miser in her tiny *buksa*, to splurge on an irresistible lollipop or sweetmeat. Meru remembered the gift she'd bought with those savings for her friend Zaitoon. A soft brocade tablecloth with embroidery and a dancing fringe. Sakina *Khala* had loved it very much as well.

'Thank you, Zaitoon!' she murmured gratefully as her

friend sat down beside her on the swing.

Meru was surprised to see the green gram sitting on the tray. She had never known them to be a breakfast item. 'Why these?' she asked curiously.

'Oh, this has been my routine for a long time. Every morning, I wake up early to help *Ammi* with her morning activities, after which I boil some gram to have as part of my ritual for inner cleansing. It is my thing actually! I mash some for *Ammi* too. I believe it has some magic. Every day I pray for her to get better. I try as much as I can so she can recover quickly.' Zaitoon pressed her lips together sadly, her expression sombre.

But she soon shook off her melancholic air and said, 'And of course, these dates are to break our fast. You know that right?'

Meru smiled at her friend's innocence and her love for her mother. Indeed, it was a huge task for Zaitoon to manage everything single-handedly.

'That's so nice, Zaitoon. You've grown so much! So mature. Where did you learn these practices?'

'Well, I've been reading my grandfather's book and it helps me stay inspired and interested in life.'

'Really?' Meru was intrigued at once and wanted to know more.

'Yes...I draw encouragement from its pages. You know, I began reading it just recently. In fact, the very reason I'm here is because of my grandfather. He left us this house as our inheritance from him. *Ammi* and I still can't believe this treasure belongs to us. We don't even know how he built this wonderful building in the first place. That too, in this prolific city of Otto! It remains a mystery.

But Meru, he specifically mentioned in his *will* that he'd like us to spend our lives here. When we came, we found he had only three possessions, wrapped in a cotton bag – a *tasbih* (rosary), a small bottle of *attar* (fragrance), and a beautiful *journal*, in which he wrote during the time he was alone. So, since we moved, I have been reading the journal. It feels good.'

'What is the book called, Zaitoon?'

'*365 Days of a Sufi.*'

'Wow! Would it be possible for me to read it too?'

'Of course. Certainly!'

'But wait! I almost forgot that I don't know how to read. I have never been to school,' she confessed, her eyes lowered in shame and sadness. The glad light suddenly went out of Meru's eyes and her head drooped.

'Do not fret, my friend, I will read it to you.' Zaitoon extended an arm and took Meru's hand in a warm clasp. 'We'll read together. It will be such fun! We will start reading from the very beginning of the book, the Prologue.'

The girls giggled with excitement. What a wonderful opportunity had come knocking at their door!

❧

CHAPTER 6

365 Days of a Sufi

Prologue

I write sitting in a place for seekers, the name of which a murshid or murid must not pronounce. It is not a secret nor is it forbidden, but it is said that the revelation of the place is whispered in the ears of only those who are ready to set their foot towards Allah. I pray the next whisper comes to you. Inshallah!

Someone here asked me if I had to tell my story to one person, who would that be? And to me, the answer was as clear as the sky is after a storm, just as the presence of Allah is everywhere — my little granddaughter, the apple of my eye, my angel — Zaitoon!

Some people think, I live in a place known as 'the town of lost souls'. Rather, it is a town of seekers, where lost souls find solace. Some say those who live here gain extraordinary wisdom and the inner eye to see things.

Well, I am just a little speck of dust. For me, it is just the beginning. Beginning of telling these extraordinary stories.

o

One day, a broken-hearted sceptic was taken to a Sufi. Many had found solace there. The man told the Sufi that he and his wife argued every single day. There was no trust between them, only misunderstanding, anger and resentment. He shared that he had four little children, yet he had gone through a long period of separation from his family. He had shifted to another town. The separation period convinced the couple that it would be best if they went their own ways. But, due to the efforts of their families, divorce did not happen. Instead, reconciliation did and they were living together once again. Yet he felt miserable. The shock of separation persisted within him and he was consumed by melancholy. The man begged the Sufi to help him in his agony.

To this, the Sufi merely said, 'Dear One, I understand your pain fully.'

The man looked at the Sufi doubtfully. 'How can you understand my suffering and pain, let alone fully?'

The Sufi smiled. 'Dear Man of God, what kind of relationship do you think I have with my Beloved?'

Yes, our relationship with Allah is quite like that of a man and wife. There is love, there is anger, and there is separation. And there is reconciliation. Yet, even with reconciliation, the heart still feels hurt and broken, deep within.

Just as we cannot share the same kind of relationship with everyone on this planet, our relationship with Allah can never be confined to just one specific kind. Have you noticed how different we are each day, even with ourselves? Living alone has given me a chance to experience my relationship with myself differently. With time, I realized I have become more gentle, kind with myself, more humble. And as I grow more into that space, I am becoming gentler and calmer, and less resentful of God.

The man asked the Sufi, 'So what did you do about your suffering?'

The Sufi replied, 'I went to my Master and shared with him my pain. I asked him if he could tell me what to do about it? He looked into my eyes and said that he would give me the solution only if I could answer one question honestly: 'Are you ready to love MORE?'

365 Days of a Sufi is thus a tale of the many simple human beings who taught me to love MORE. My life has led me to a Pandora's Box of secrets, which I am about to tell you. Secrets that have led me to believe in the magic of love, which is found nowhere but within. In my time of living alone, I realized that I had to be alone not to know Allah, but humans. In that aloneness, I connected with every human and through every human, with Allah in each one.

My friend, it is not new to human thought that we are all Children of God, but to feel that way is another story altogether. It isn't new that there is light within each one of us, but to be in its effulgent rays is unfathomable. It isn't new that we will all merge into Allah one day, but to actually experience that while still alive is ...

Ibne-Al-Rashid, 5 June 1899

CHAPTER 7

It was nearly evening and the sun had begun to tone down its fire. The breeze felt soothing as it passed whispering by. The shoals of people on the streets seemed to be dispersing to go home to prayers and supper. A bell clanged in the home, its brassy sound carrying over its walls. It was followed by a brief wave of children's chatter.

Meru was alone on the terrace, soaking in all the sights and sounds. Zaitoon had accompanied her *Ammi* to a *hakim*, well-known in the precinct, for her regular check-up. Meru felt wildly alone in that big house. Indeed, it wasn't hers. When alone in her own home, she had often slept on the only cot, where her *Ammi* and *Abu* had slept, for some solace. Being alone in one's own house was one thing, but being alone in someone else's space seemed enormous, fierce even. It pierced her. The loneliness she had felt so often before, now seemed like a strange presence in this new space.

And as she sat in that vacuum, Meru could not help contemplating Zaitoon's world. Zaitoon was educated, knew a foreign language, was far more beautiful than Meru, and still had the love of her mother. In fact, she had everything she needed to lead a contented life.

Meru was pained to see her own sorrow and grief emerge from the ravine of her heart; emotions she had learned to bury deep within, and continue to live. Zaitoon had so much more than her. Meru's petulant thoughts continued to groove gravely in her mind. She was irked by her own envy. She wondered if she had erred on accepting this invitation.

Her mind meandering, Meru lifted a leg and rested her foot on the elevated parapet of the terrace. She bent to look down at the busy street and then raised her head skyward. The openness of the world and the vast space around her felt different, perhaps more free.

Yet it suffocated her. Feeling harried, she quickly turned and ran into the house, pushed open the door to a tiny store room, and shut herself up. The room was smaller than even her home in Bashirbagh.

That comforted her. That darkness inside, she was used to. She wanted to feel that closeness of the walls she always knew. The tightness of that space helped her flee the limitlessness of freedom she was experiencing within. She wanted to stop experiencing herself crossing the boundaries of her heart and the mind. There, she felt comfortable. Easy! Tears helped her to settle in with this familiarity.

CHAPTER 8

'Why don't you two go out to the market, Zaitoon?' *Ammi* suggested, her speech a bit slurred still, the words a little crooked. There was no doubt that Meru had become deeply attached to Sakina *Khala* in the few days she had been in the big house. In Sakina, Meru saw a reflection of her own mother.

'You must take Meru there. Buy her some nice things; whatever she likes,' Sakina managed to complete the sentence slowly, saliva drooling from one corner of her mouth.

'Certainly, *Ammi!*' Zaitoon responded and gently dabbed the cruelly bent lips with a soft handkerchief. Lovingly, she pushed *Ammi's* bristly grey hair behind her ears saying, 'It's time to rest.' She pulled a coverlet over *Ammi's* shoulders, and caressing one cheek said, 'We'll go out in a while. It is Friday – a good day. You sleep now. We will lock the door.'

'Don't worry about us,' Meru said, sitting beside the charpoy and holding Sakina's hand. 'I'm so happy just to be here and to spend time with you both. *Khala*, if there is anything I can do for you, please tell me. I will be very happy to be of help.'

Sakina smiled, comforted by the care of both the girls. 'You may call me *Ammi*, child,' she said.

Meru's heart thudded. In that moment she felt invited, loved and cared for. Her doubts about her visit to Otto, faded away. Gently, she took *Khala's* palm and kissed it, murmuring, '*Ammi*'. But Sakina's eyelids were already weighted down in sleep.

Zaitoon wiped *Ammi's* face once again and planted a kiss on her forehead.

○

The walk in the market was nothing less than an adventure for Meru. The main town square was often filled with visitors from nearby towns and cities. One saw flocks of tourists from other parts of the world too, who sat in the stylish cafés and eateries that encircled the colossal central fountain. The clattering of porcelain cups and bowls, and the aroma of ground beans and brewed teas, suffused the air with a refreshing scent.

Meru was fascinated to see clothes of all kinds, both traditional and modern. Colourful *keffiyehs*, *salwars*, headscarfs, *lehengas*, dresses with embroidered sleeves, pleated skirts, and harem pants with batik prints, silken drapes and chiffon *dupattas*. Clothing from many cultures hung in an appealing, ubiquitous mix. The lanterns, carpets, chandeliers, drapes, left the girls speechless. There were trinkets, accessories made of beads and stones and precious metals. And out of all the variety of footwear, Meru adored the blue soft sandals the best. There were vendors of aromatic spices who were calling out to their customers in peculiar rhythmic tunes, throwing in exotic descriptions of each spice.

Across the square stood a stretch of dry fruits, sweets and nuts' stalls. Pistachio, almonds, fox-nuts, walnuts, hazelnuts – all in heaped bulk. Meru learned from Zaitoon that many traders from the neighbouring desert towns and villages, with their caravans, regularly came to this market with their wares. Meru had never seen anything like it; the colours had never looked more enticing!

She was struck by the stark contrast between where she stood and the market where she had gone to work for years. The two couldn't be seamed together. The bazaars of Bashirbagh had fewer shops and were anything but flamboyant. The offerings were limited – clothes and vessels, meat, shoes and umbrellas. A few vendors sold grains, vegetables and spices. It was like an old fading painting where the colours had lost their sheen and people had forgotten their enthusiasm.

Suddenly, Meru's eyes fell on something familiar – a shine she had known all her life. They were standing near a *zari* weaving workshop, where scarves, kameez and fabrics of all kinds, with *zari* work on them, were on display. She peeped inside and saw weavers sitting on the mattresses with their legs folded under them, eyes focussed and fingers adeptly working the fine gold and silver threads. Watching them work on such a variety of intricate designs was a source of delight for her eyes and heart. 'Such discipline...such artistry...' Meru murmured in appreciation.

Zaitoon was amused to see the twinkle in Meru's eyes as she stood transfixed and beguiled, gazing in turn at each weaver, working shiny threads into the corner of the fabric they held. Indeed, Meru was a *zari* weaver too!

'Meru…' she said, curious to know more about her friend, 'where did you learn *zari* weaving?'

Eyes still fixed on threads and fingers, Meru said, 'You know Zaitoon, this is the only kind of work that I have ever known.' She paused and looked up at her friend thoughtfully. 'But there are only certain kinds of patterns that my brain knows how to weave. I did the work simply to make money. It was a matter of survival. If I could choose, I would love to study the art much more closely. I am enthralled by these designs. I was always instructed on what designs to make. It was standard work. Although I did experiment with a few of my original designs on some orders, they were sparse.'

'But the style you weave is known as the Bashirbagh style,' Zaitoon said. 'Does weaving limited designs bother you?'

Meru heaved a long sigh. She had never given it much thought, until this moment. 'Zaitoon, I have no idea what I'm doing here on this planet. My life revolved around my parents, and between those two streets. I never knew what existed beyond them till I came to your house. In a few days, I realized what I'd missed in so many years.' Meru paused again.

As they resumed their walk in the market, she let out another small sigh before saying, 'I always kept myself busy. But in reality, my life has been in a blank state. I have no idea when I was born – which month, which date. I don't even know what my real age is. I have learned to live like this. Yet I have often wondered why this *zari* work came to me and not something else? *Ammi* and *Abu* considered it to be sacred work though. In olden times, *zari* was used exclusively for gifting. Taking *zari* clothes to someone's house was considered the same as bringing the presence of *Allah*. Knowing this art and doing this work was believed to be pure and holy. I used to wonder if this explanation was true. So I came up with my own answer – that perhaps *Allah* wanted people to wear it, and that way know that *Allah* resides in all. Time and again my parents reminded me that this was the best thing to do in the world. And that made me feel worthwhile and good.'

☙

CHAPTER 9

365 Days of a Sufi

Month One

One day, a Sufi sat down to meditate at his usual time. He was quite diligent with his practice and an ardent lover of *Allah*. His only dream was to meet his Beloved once and merge with the Divine. He had been on several journeys to experience this love for his Beloved, and to express his heart's devotion.

On that day as he was about to close his eyes to begin his meditation, when there was an unexpected knock on the door. Perplexed, he looked up.

'Who is it?'

'God,' came the answer from the other side.

'It is time for my meditation,' answered the Sufi, and closed his eyes.

Such is the life of a simple man.

What comes knocking at your door? A new friend, a new human, a new house, a new time, a new situation, a new opportunity, a new sign? And yet, we are so accustomed to our old life that it is hard for us humans to give ourselves that little space for the love of newness. We cannot make extra room for it. The new in our lives is like a guest who has just arrived as a surprise.

Always keep a guest room ready inside you. What if one day, the one you are seeking actually arrives and needs a place to reside in you? Make space. Tidy the room and make it holy. We certainly need to give our guests some extra comfort, until they get used to the ways of our abode. As we adjust to the guest, the guest will do so too. Our new self is that guest who arrives.

Give love to the new. It needs attention. Just as a new pet in the house, or a newborn baby, needs extra attention and care, so does our new self. When a new turn shows up in our lives, it is a new journey that our being must venture on, so walk with it. Hold its hand. Love it.

There is another way to look at the Sufi's story.

The Sufi is so close to Allah inside himself, that he doesn't feel the need to meet Him outside. Thus, love resides inside you. Get used to that love. Connect with the heart. In-between those heartbeats is the dose of extra love that needs pumping and life.

Ultimately, everything put on this planet is for you.

PART II

CHAPTER 10

The child in Zaitoon never knew childhood, and the adult in Meru never grew up. There was a void of experience between the two friends. So, though Zaitoon was happy being with Meru, she missed her presence despite being with her. She couldn't find the solace and understanding she needed from a friend. Usually, Meru was quiet and aloof, almost an inscrutable presence in the room. It was only when Zaitoon asked her something that Meru responded.

Meru, on the other hand, would have loved to talk but she didn't know what to say. She was caught up in her own sense of identity reformation. Watching the diversity of the city unfold before her eyes, the different culture and unfamiliar norms, she felt there was always more in the world that she wasn't introduced to, before. To Meru, Zaitoon seemed to be in a better place, and liberated.

But Zaitoon had her own set of challenges. She almost envied Meru's life and freedom. Many a time, emotion would suffocate her as she watched her mother struggle for minuscule things. And every alternate day *Ammi* needed to be taken to the *hakim*. Apart from tutoring children, Zaitoon's day was consumed with endless household chores, while still trying to adapt to a new city herself.

Zaitoon was her mother's only recourse, hence she was her priority. Zaitoon had given up on her education and also made peace with sacrificing her womanly urges and desires, including leaving behind in the village a boy she had loved and wanted to marry. Her life was a juggling act between her own story and that of her mother. But she never reproached anyone, nor complained about it.

Zaitoon often remembered her *Abba*, who disappeared one night and never returned. Many claimed that he, like his learned and holy father, Ibne-al-Rashid, went to find his solace in *Allah*, while others claimed he had abandoned his family for another woman, the shock of which had caused Sakina's paralysis. Which version was true Zaitoon did not know, but what she knew and remembered was that her *Abba* had always wanted her to complete her *talim* and be a learned woman.

Though elated at being reunited with her childhood friend, having Meru in her house also felt like raising a child. Meru was overwhelmed by the world that was changing so rapidly around her. Inside, there was great freedom, yet untapped. And she had never crossed paths with love, nor had anyone asked for love from her.

$$\mathcal{L}$$

CHAPTER 11

365 Days of a Sufi

Month Two

One day I was alone at home. Well, I am always alone. But that day was unusual, for a stranger, a woman, came into the house without knocking. At first, I was astonished, and perhaps somewhat afraid of the stranger. But then I thought that perhaps she had come here by mistake. That she was in the wrong house, or needed something desperately.

She looked at me with her gimlet eyes and sat down on the floor. I did not know whether I was in some dream or awake. Somehow, I chose to remain silent. Catching her breath, she stood up, went to the kitchen, drank some water, and then left.

I was alarmed, but as the day passed, I forgot about it. The next day, she came again. This time, she brought a five or six-year-old boy with her. Once again she went to the kitchen, drank some water, gave some to the child, and then went away. This time, she didn't even stare at me.

How on earth could someone do this and I let it happen? Why couldn't I stop the woman from entering my home? Wary of her intrusive presence, I thought I should keep the door latched. But then, in the evening, when I opened the door to go to the market, I saw her marching towards my house with many children in tow, and this time she also carried a baby in her arms. Not looking at me, she entered the house, the children following, and they all drank water. Now I felt annoyed. So, as she was about to leave with the children, I gathered up the courage to stop her and ask who she was and what she was doing. Where were those children from? And how did she so casually enter my home?

She looked at me this time, her eyes subdued. In them, I saw a million stories and struggles embedded. Her eyes clearly reflected the purity of her heart; her honesty. She said in a clear guileless voice, 'So am I forbidden to drink water from your earthen pot?'

I was perplexed and her question made me think. There was absolutely no reason why I shouldn't let anyone drink water from my pot.

'Will knowing who I am make the water in the pot any different? Will it make a difference to you?'

I thought about it. Certainly, it did not make any difference. She could continue drinking the water from my pot. It made no difference at all.

'Will knowing who I am make my thirst any different from yours?'

'No', I answered. Thirst is thirst. It is the same for everyone. It doesn't make any difference what stories you wear inside you.

After she had left, I realized there was no point in asking who I was either. There was no point in asking God: 'Who are you?' The fact that I had water to quench my thirst, and love inside me to quench the thirst of my soul, was enough. I didn't need permission to sip this water anywhere in the world.

Since that day, I found new meaning in waking up each morning. Each day I filled water in my pot, thinking about the woman and children. I also began to fill myself with love and did more *ibadat.* It became a peaceful love affair, between *Allah* and myself, through my *ibadat.* And every evening, the woman, along with many children, came to quench their thirst.

This continued for a long time. Neither of us knew the other. We didn't know each other's story. But we continued to do our work. I continued to fill my pot with water, and she came to drink it.

This is our relationship with Allah…

How can we not believe that the emptiness we feel within us is because Allah came to us to quench His thirst?

Thus, keep some extra pots, extra love.

Later, I came to know that the woman was a rare and ardent dervish. She showed up in the homes of God's disciples, to do her work. Rafia was her name. Her desire was to meet every lover of God, but God Himself. She wanted to meet the love that would nourish her soul and give her courage to love her God even more. Meeting the lovers created hope within her that there was more. Her Beloved was loved by many. Many more than just her!

CHAPTER 12

A little boy asked his father, 'Who is a Sufi?'

The father looked at his son and shared an anecdote with him: 'Once, there were two men who went to the Master. They asked him if he knew of a place where one could find the light of *Allah*. The Master gave them an address, and both started out on their individual journeys.

After a few days, one man returned to the Master and said he had lost his way and asked him for the address once again. But the other one never came back. The one who never came back is a Sufi.'

○

One day, a *murshid* went to Rafia, a learned woman, and asked, 'What can a human do in times of uncertainty? When you feel that you do not deserve what has knocked on your door? When there is a sudden appalling situation and irksome adversity?'

To this, Rafia responded peacefully: 'Let me tell you a story. A man marries a woman and on the first night, the woman falls down and loses her memory. Instead of getting mad or blaming fate and waiting for her memory to return, the man starts to teach his wife. Each night after work, after all the chores were done, he sat with his wife to teach her – the alphabets, words, sentences – so that she could read, write and be independent, and weave a new life. Soon, the nights were spent learning the language of love and lessons of life. Their time together became their time of wisdom; almost like poetry.'

On hearing this, the *murshid* asked curiously, 'Do you know them? What does the wife do now? I would like to meet them.'

'She is sitting in front of you dear *murshid,* and telling you her story,' replied Rafia.

$\mathcal{L}$

CHAPTER 13

Zaitoon understood that it was important to let Meru be. It didn't matter who she had become in the time they had been separated, instead she thought of the phenomenal day of their reunion.

'The first night *Ammi* and I moved here was an interesting one,' Zaitoon told Meru.

The swing on the terrace gently swung the two friends to and fro as they gazed at the stars shining over the town.

'I was scared of this big house in the beginning, of this big terrace, the high ceilings echoing my own voice. Everything was ancient, but also grand! It was difficult to accept and adjust to at first. Gradually, I began to believe that this was actually my home and not just a dream. I'd never thought in my wildest imaginings that change would come to me in this way... so drastic...so dramatic.'

'I cannot even imagine how happy you must have felt knowing your grandfather left you such a huge inheritance!' Meru exclaimed, looking at her friend and reliving her excitement.

'Yes, it was one of the happiest surprises of my life. But then I began to think that I was alone with *Ammi*. What if she were to leave me or never wake up from her sleep? I would be left all alone. Such thoughts disturbed me. They haunted me every single day. They reverberated from the very walls of this house. I could not sleep. My soul felt restless.'

Meru held Zaitoon's hand and looked into her glistening eyes. She knew perfectly how it felt to be left an orphan. How it felt to be alone. The four walls of her own small house had deepened their silence in grief and sorrow, but they were the same four walls that also gave her a sense of safety, containing the happy memories of her parents.

'Do not worry,' Meru said to her friend 'You will find the courage to stand up and walk, to be happy.'

'Meru, the day we met again, that morning I had woken up feeling extremely sad. I felt all alone in this large city. In fact, I felt *Allah* was far from me and he could not hear my voice, or my prayers. But I was so wrong. I genuinely asked for help, for support, for some hope, for some strength, for an answer. I yearned for it.' Zaitoon gave a long sigh, then continued, 'Fortunately, I found an answer the same day. The answer was you!' Zaitoon turned her gaze upon Meru, her demure best friend.

On hearing this, Meru's eyes lit up. Deep down, she felt valued and worthy. She knew Zaitoon really loved her and her words made Meru feel sated with reassurance.

Holding one of Meru's hands, Zaitoon continued, 'It is true. I was so chuffed to see you at the shop. You know, that day, out of the blue, *Ammi* handed me a piece of raw silk I'd never seen before. It looked expensive. She asked if we could get some *zari* work done on it, so I could wear it for *Ramadan*. I went to the town square, hoping to find a *zari* weaving shop that would not be exorbitant. But everything in Otto is mighty pricey.

After visiting many merchants, someone referred me to the owner of your shop, telling me that his work was decent and it would be within my budget. It took me a while to figure out the alleys and bazaar of Bashirbagh, and the tiny shops, but then there you were! I had never thought we'd meet again! All these years I thought that you too must have migrated somewhere like we did, or got married; become a mother even. *Ha ha.* I believe there is a reason why certain things happen. I'm so happy you happened to me again, Meru.' Zaitoon's face radiated the joy in her heart.

A mellow breeze continued to carry the fragrance of the flowers in the little pots around them. On the horizon, a thicket of maple and sycamore trees rested in the arms of the mountains, and the moon hid shyly behind the moving clouds.

'Meru, do you feel the same? I hope you are equally happy to meet me?' Zaitoon asked anxiously.

'Zaitoon, of course I'm happy. Very happy!' Meru exclaimed. 'In fact for me, the morning we met began like any other – I cleaned my house, washed clothes, made a meal for the day, had tea, and left for work. While I was busy weaving at the shop, Gulfam *Kaka* suddenly came up to me and asked if I could take care of the shop till the evening, while he was away. This was a rare thing. I have worked with him for years, and he has immense trust in me, but he never left the shop entirely to me, until sundown. He said that his daughter was visiting and his grandson insisted on going to the *Kabutarkhana* in a particular park, to feed the birds. Gulfam *Kaka* wanted to go out to buy the seed, which was not sold in our neighbourhood. I suppose, he surely must have come to the bazaars of Otto. Inquisitive,

I asked what the park was called and guess what he said? Zaitoon Park!'

'Really?' Zaitoon was both elated and amused by the strange coincidence.

'And then he told me a little of the history of the park. Long ago, an old man living on the streets, had a fascination for birds and animals. He used the alms he received to buy grains to feed the birds. It made him happy. People started to notice his gesture and felt great warmth and kindness towards him. That is how he became the seed that kindled generosity in people. When he died, people continued to feed the birds in memory of his legacy of kindness. Hence the name *Zaitoon*, meaning *seed*.

Listening to Gulfam *Kaka*, I made up my mind to someday visit the park myself and feed the birds too. But I didn't have to wait for long. A different seed happened to me that day. You!' Meru said joyfully. 'It didn't just happen out of the blue, Zaitoon. It was a sign. I am sure of it.'

The night was deepening but the city was bathed in passing moonlight as the bloated, woozy clouds swept across the sky. Pindrop silence had fallen on the earth but the two friends could not stop harking back to their earlier days. Their lives seemed to have been adorned with each other's presence.

'I pray that our friendship grows forever,' Zaitoon said at last. She could see a new composure arising in her friend, something she had never seen before. It felt promising.

The two childhood friends were grateful for each other's company and the shared solitude. They went on swinging and talking late into the night, lost in a joyful world of their own.

'Zaitoon, I really want to know more about your grandfather and his life.'

It was true. Meru always listened raptly to the stories Zaitoon read to her from the journal.

'Me too...' murmured Zaitoon.

ꝭ

CHAPTER 14

365 Days of a Sufi

Month Three

I am from a simple family. We were seven siblings in all. Although I was the eldest, I was the most playful one and had no inclination for growing up too soon. I was curious and had a deep admiration for everything around me. I was happy to be born and grateful to be able to experience so many beguiling things. Life always seemed alluring to me. But that phase proved to be short-lived. When my father passed away, the responsibility of nurturing my siblings for their lives ahead was on my shoulders. I had no notion what I was supposed to do. Our mother too had passed away quite early, and I had no idea what life truly was. I was very naïve, never having experienced any setbacks closely enough. I tackled situations on the basis of my feelings rather than reasoning.

On his deathbed, my father asked me to go and see his dear friend in Pena, a famous but distant city. I had, of course, never been to Pena, but I knew many people went there in pursuit of their dreams. It was certainly a big deal to be a resident of Pena, but nowhere was it within the radar of my imagination. It seemed just a far-fetched dream, not meant for me.

My father's friend was supposedly a very rich man. I knew absolutely nothing about him until my father's last breath. He had never spoken of him. My father simply asked me to meet this friend, and that was it. All I knew was his name – Musa. There was no address, just Pena…

I sold my bicycle to arrange some money for the long journey. It was important for me to complete this task. I was just 17 then. But then, I was also resolute and fastidious. For days and nights, I travelled through the big and small towns to reach the city of dreams. My thirsting heart again felt admiration for every little thing, as I was reaching closer and closer to Pena. Far in distance, I saw two crimson minarets. They beckoned to me irresistibly, holding all the allure of a holy creation of *Allah*.

Pena was indeed a mesmerising place, with art and beauty in every corner; a hub of creative and intellectual people. The city was home to many legends – both those who had been born there, and those who had come from afar to make it their home; forever consumed by the love and wisdom of nature. There were large public libraries built by scholars, and I had heard about the student gatherings in the evenings, to listen to the masters, scholars and teachers discussing all manner of subjects. Such an outpouring of knowledge would have been impossible in the small town where I lived. Many artists came to find their way to void or victory in this city. Many poets were born, and poetry is what they left behind for eternity; some inscribed on the great walls of public edifices. Outside one of the *konaks* called *Hayati*, at the city entrance, I read on a wall these words, which I can never forget:

There are two worlds inside me. One is of poetry, and another lost. When the two meet, they perhaps understand each other. Sometimes, the poetry sings to the lost, and at other times the lost takes the poetry to places it got lost in. And in their camaraderie, they both find themselves. Just momentarily. That is the world of us, the hayati!

It is hard to describe the beauty of Pena. There were wise old trees with massive trunks and expansive branches, park benches planted on scenic routes and around ponds, and little eateries at every corner. The roads were cobalt and the architecture was of historical significance. Every evening, people gathered at the city fountains, surrounded by local markets and cafés. The city had several bridges, with gurgling streams flowing under them, and wide-open spaces and prairies where people came to soak in the warmth of the sun. There were also quiet and lean streets branching out from many curbs, some like a labyrinth. Pena was certainly a place plumed by its own beauty. One cannot behold the sight of magpies crossing a rose-pink sky.

The market had fresh exotic fruits and vegetables of all colours and shapes, some I had never seen before. Artefacts made from wood, clay, granite, and even copper, showed the city's rich artistic heritage. There were gardens with fountains and green lawns, where children played and young people read, wrote and painted. Freestanding *sabil* and kiosks with mosaic tiles and ceramic designs were to be found everywhere, where attendants offered water through the grilled windows; a way of serving the people. To me, Pena looked like a perfect rendition of God's creation. Naturally, I was smitten and immediately resolved to move to this beautiful city someday.

Meanwhile, though I had a purpose to fulfil, I was determined to find my father's friend. I was also driven by this mystical curiosity. Why did my father ask me to meet his old friend after all these years? Nearly everyone I spoke to knew who he was, but no one could direct me to him. Until one day a man pointed me to a person sitting on a gunny bag on a street corner, with his eyes closed. He had a long beard and was clothed in rags and tatters. I thought it improbable that he was the man I was looking for. Nonetheless, I walked towards him and waited for him to open his eyes.

'Musa?' I asked hesitantly when his eyes opened.

He looked at me and smiled. I was surprised by that affectionate look and decorous gesture.

'I knew you'd come. You are the late Hyder's son!' he exclaimed in his soft yet deep voice. He opened his palms, looked towards the sky and said a small prayer.

'His soul is in peace.'

'*Aameen!*' I bowed in respect. 'Yes, I am his son,' I stood there, bewildered.

I still remember that moment clearly. When I was approaching that man, all my thoughts stopped, unknowingly. A gentle breeze touched my face and my steps slowed their pace and became steadier, as if I were entering a holy place. I felt pure peace in my heart. All my questions seemed to vanish. My mind stopped swaying and became more centred.

I can now say that this was my first brush with mysticism, or rather, a subtle introduction to it.

My heart was melting. Under those rags was someone who knew life way beyond what my senses could decipher. Now I knew what my father had meant when he told me Musa had a treasure. In that moment, I too, had my first realization of who I was. I wasn't just a 17-year-old boy on the cusp of early manhood, but an intensely thirsty and curious soul who wished to walk the same path as this man called Musa, about whom I knew nothing. His appearance could be deceptive but his existence was sheer poetry.

'Come, sit next to me,' he said.

I must be dreaming! I thought to myself. Though I felt rather embarrassed to sit down with him on the street, I really wanted to know what this mystic had in store for me.

'My name is Rashid,' I pronounced, bowing my head, hand on my heart. A new kind of humility and respect were building a home within me.

He smiled and nodded, implying that he knew it.

'*Abba* said you have a treasure.' My innocence was prompt in revealing itself.

He looked right into my eyes; the depth of his gaze was beyond me.

'Your *Abba* had the same treasure. Didn't you see it?' he asked, his eyes still transfixed on mine.

Even those piercing eyes felt gentle and his nod, benign. However, his question perforated my young mind. Perplexed, I tried to recollect all the little things *Abba* had ever done or told me.

'No,' I said gravely, 'he never showed it to me or told me about it.'

'Hmmm…' Musa went into deep thought and receded into a prolonged pause.

Everything in that moment seemed so mysterious, so unreal. I could not move.

Finally, he rose. 'Come, let me take you to that place then.'

○

It was a silent, placid lake. The water seemed frozen in time, unmoving. It was where Musa and Hyder, my father, first met and became friends, where they had looked in awed admiration at the monumental palace that stood magnificently in the centre of the lake.

The palace was a city landmark. Iconic indeed! Hundreds of visitors came every day just to gaze at this majestic palace, shining amidst stars and lights. Each night, thousands of lamps would be lit outside this imperial palace, and little lighted boats would float upon the lake, making a breath-taking sight. With the changing phases of the moon, the palace's beauty shone, bride-like. It was glorious on a full moon night, each adornment visible to those who looked. On the night of the crescent moon, it was an intriguing hide-and-seek of shadow and light. It was as though God had come to worship his own worshippers. Indeed, my words fell short in describing its regal existence.

'Hyder was sitting at the very spot you are now,' Musa said to me as he sat dipping his feet in the cold water. The water purled around his ankles. The lake was calm and tranquil though the wind ruffled our hair and tugged playfully at his beard. The wide-open sky looked splendid. The gargantuan entrance to the palace seemed enigmatic.

Eventually, Musa began to share the story of his remarkable time with my father, a tale that ignited a fire in me to embark on a similar journey.

I knew I had to write about what I heard...one day. And so it came to pass. And what a joy it is to write it when I too, am on the same journey. So let me call this part of my journal *Musa's Tales* – true stories, as recounted to me by Musa himself.

CHAPTER 15

Musa's Tales

'I saw him in the wee hours of the morning, when I was on my regular walk. I had never seen him before, and I wondered who this tall slim young man was, who in silence, was exuberating poise and a disarming sweetness of life? There was no one else around.

Hours passed in silence. But then, as the sun was about to make its first stroke in the sky, I heard him whistle. It was a melody unknown to me and it echoed in the absolute silence of the dawn. I didn't know it then, but it was the harbinger of our holy friendship. He went on whistling as the sky changed its colour from deep blue to pink to shades of crimson and magenta. I was intrigued by how his melodies changed with the shifting hues of the sky. I couldn't stop myself from probing.

'Wow! You whistle well. That's a beautiful tune. Where did you learn it?'

He turned to look at where the voice had come from. He saw me, stood up, and walked towards me, still whistling, as if answering me with those sounds. He sat down next to me, as if he knew me and I knew him, and that serene lake, the ageless sky and the colossal palace, were our common friends since a million lives.

Looking up, I could see the birds swooping to his tunes in the sky. It was a windy morning and the rustle of leaves blended with the tune. Little multi-coloured butterflies fluttered around. This went on till the sun rose from behind the palace. Then he stopped whistling and sighed. He looked at me, his unusual ocean-blue eyes shining deep. We broke into laughter, and just like that we became friends.

He put a hand on my shoulder and said, 'Thank you, my friend.'

'The delight is mine. You just made my morning come alive!' I said.

'I am Hyder.'

'I'm Musa. So what brings you here?'

'My life!' he answered simply.

Instantly, I felt a special connection with him; his answer intrigued me. 'What do you mean by that?' I asked.

'Isn't it simple? My life brought me here,' he stated.

Smiling at my puzzled face, he went on as if he were merely picking up our conversation from where we had left it last. It was so simple with him. Easy...yet not. He was some years older than me, probably in his late twenties, yet he had charmed me with his candour and precocious mannerisms.

'I'm on an apprenticeship,' he said.

'Apprenticeship?' That both intrigued and perplexed me.

'A few years ago, I decided to seek initiation on the path of the Sufi. So I travelled to the pilgrim city of the *dervish*, called Asmaar, to seek my abode in the holy place of *Allah*. I was thirsty for knowledge. I attended many *sama, sohebet,* and *dhikr*. Then, one day, I thought I was so ready to be initiated on the path that I decided to meet the Master and become his apprentice. Alas, it wasn't that easy. I was given a *chilla*, on the completion of which, I would be considered to be initiated as an apprentice.'

'What is *chilla?*' I asked. The sun had almost shown all its rays by then.

'*Chillas* are sacred tasks. Some take a few minutes, and some a lifetime to accomplish. New followers like me are given these tasks. Some are asked to go on a solitary journey for forty days, maybe to a cave or the desert or some solitary place. Some, are asked to go to an orphanage and serve the children there; some are asked to speak to homeless people living on the streets and spend time with them; others are told to fast and do *bandagi*. Some are given a series of practices and thesis and poetry to study and learn.'

'What are your sacred tasks and for how long?' I asked, riveted by what he told me.

'I am on my sacred tasks right now. The Master told me to keep journeying around the world and wait until something significant happened. This event would bring me to a point when I would have to decide whether I wished to return to Asmaar for initiation or not. That moment will come, I was told. Yet, my friend, I have no idea when that moment and that point will arrive, or what the event will be.'

'Are you not scared, Hyder? What if it takes your whole lifetime?' I felt harried by the thought.

'You see, a few days ago I was about to end my life,' Hyder said matter-of-factly and continued, 'I was deeply depressed and grieving. An undefined, unknown void rested as a seed in my heart. At the time, I was living on a pavement. Others like me suffered the winter cold, an empty stomach, a roofless earth, and the unmerciful rain. For days I spoke to no one. Those others were strangers to me, I thought; as I was to them. But that wasn't true. A ragged man looked at my wan face and sordid state one day and asked if I was okay? I broke down. For a long time I had not heard a human voice talk to me, let alone express concern.

'I feel like giving up,' I said to him, quivering with fresh, restless thoughts.

'What do you have that you want to give up?' the stranger asked.

'In that question, I found the answer. What did I have that I wanted to give up? I repeated the question in my mind. *I actually have nothing!* A voice came from my heart and woke me up to life again.'

'Take your life somewhere,' he said, as if he had heard my realization; as if he had been sent by my Master.

He saw something in me that I thought I was incapable of. He smiled gently, his eyes fixed on mine. 'Have you observed a baby's life? A baby cannot sit still. The mother takes her restless curious baby out with her to so many places. They look at beautiful things, meet different people. The entire world is defined for the child by the mother's eyes. They see the sunrise, the moon, animals, plants etc. So take yourself somewhere else. Go from here!'

I looked at him transfixed.

'You know,' he continued, '*Allah* is in everyone. Not at any one place but everywhere.'

And then he said something that turned my world around.

'Take that *Allah* everywhere with you!'

Part of me felt so responsible. If *Allah* dwelt inside me, like that baby with his mother, then I needed to take the little one with me, to see the world out there. However, I didn't know if, like that mother, I had the prowess to define the world to *Allah*. So I started my journey once again. And here I am now, staring at this world-famous palace in the middle of Lake Pena!'

I was keenly listening to this incredible young man, Hyder, humbly unravelling his journey. 'So what do you think of the palace, my friend?' I asked.

He looked at the palace with his winsome gaze. 'I can adore its beauty from the shore, but I cannot go in there,' he posited. 'It isn't my palace. *Allah* seems to be like that too. He is at the centre of my heart but I certainly don't own it. The reason I whistle is to converse with and express my love to Allah. I know that in this way my yearning will reach him, no matter how far I am yet from initiation.'

'Would you like to see what's inside that *Allah*?' I quickly asked him and this time it was Hyder who looked bewildered.

CHAPTER 16

'That is my palace,' I told him matter-of-factly.

'You must be joking!' Hyder said, baffled.

'No, it is true. Come, let me take you on a visit.'

He didn't move, remaining rapt in the beaming beauty of the palace. I asked him what was on his mind and once again his answer amazed me.

'The palace looks stunning from this distance,' he said. 'What if I pine for this beauty once I go in?'

'What makes you think so?' I asked.

His gaze remained steady upon the magnificent structure before him. The lake was the sky itself, shining in the sunlight. The sharp rays lay incandescent on the lake. He immersed his feet in the water and let the waves kiss them gently. He seemed determined not to move.

'But you know, we will come back here,' I said, insisting.

He shook his head. 'Now is not the time. Let me soak in this first. What happens next will be a different time altogether, with different choices. That man on the street told me one more thing: *Let the present be complete. Very soon it will become the past. And an incomplete past is likely to confuse, even rule you.*'

He sat there for hours in stillness until he finally said, 'Okay, now I am ready to go in. Let's go!'

What he said about the *present* and the *past* had triggered some nervousness in my heart. He will certainly go away and I will never see him again, ever. I was already feeling the agony of him departing after our visit to the palace. He was a seeker, a rover, a true lover of God. Agreed, he was on a journey, but my heart was wretched with the exacerbating thought of his leaving. I didn't want to feel the misery of losing this wonderful friendship. My own vulnerable heart surprised me.

With these mixed feelings, I invited Hyder to sit with me in the boat that was moored nearby, so that we could row to the palace. That excited him. I could see the childlike glint in his eyes. They seemed so fresh and magnetic as if he was just freshly born, raw out of the womb, new to this whole world. He told me that ever since he had started on his *chilla,* all his experiences had been serendipitous.

CHAPTER 17

Musa's Tales

The boat ride across the lake to the palace is still so clear in my memory. Hyder was silent, observing me row the boat and looking at the swans that kept swimming towards us. He smiled at every little thing. He listened intently to the swishing sound of the oars slicing through the water, and the infinite ripples they made. In that moment, he gathered everything there was to gather.

'Would you like to row, Hyder?' I asked him.

He kept looking at me as he considered my question. 'No. Sometimes, it is good to let someone hold you and take you along to your destination.'

I smiled and continued to row. Wisps of thoughts rose in my mind as to how audaciously this man had left behind all his belongings to get closer to *Allah*, just like I was pushing this oar against the water so our boat would move forward. As we got closer to the palace, I kept thinking that had Hyder not left the pavement and fought off his despondency, he would not have reached Pena; nor would I have had the grace of meeting him.

From the corner of his eye he seemed to speculate on the shore we had left behind to get to where we were going. His gestures kept me inquisitive. In his presence, my own parched heart felt moored to his wisdom. I had been to the shore so many times. I had rowed that little boat so many times, but it was not till that day that I could look at life's metaphors so distinctly. For me, the boat and the rowing were just a means of going to and fro, nothing else. Hyder, on the other hand, saw meaning in everything.

○

First, we rowed to *Kabootar Khana*, also known as *Chota Mahal* to the residents of Pena. It was a small open-domed structure held up with four pillars, carved with the poetry and *qawwalis* of eminent poets. The *Kabootar Khana* was connected by a small promenade to the main palace, accessible only to those who lived in the palace. Hyder looked at the pigeons and many other species of birds, some pecking, some resting under the eaves gently, and some huddling towards him and settling on his shoulders, outstretched arms and head. Hyder chuckled with excitement. There were a number of peacocks dancing, showing off their colourful plumage. Ducks and geese splayed in the lake.

'I have been feeding the birds since I was a little child,' I told him. 'It has been a ritual for me; a very valued one these days. It gives me peace to be with them, to listen to the flutter of their wings and their cooing, and to watch them take free flight under the iridescent sky. I love to watch them eagerly rush to me and hurriedly peck at the grains I offer them.

A few years ago, I stood here with my father, feeding the birds one morning. That day, my mind kept going back to one thought – the grain I held in my hands, did not belong to me. Of course, I held the grain, but I had not earned it.

Everything around here belonged to my father. He made all this. Each grain had his name written on it. Maybe it was just the fleeting thought of a callow youth. But no.... the thought only served to pose more questions, prying into my life.'

Hyder was still glancing around, taking in all the sights and the sounds. But I knew he was listening to me intently. So I told him, 'I was happy to be a part of this world that my father had created. But somewhere within, my heart also longed to identify with something that was made by me; something I had poured my soul into. I felt the urge to create something of my own. So I shared my honest thoughts with my father, to which he said exactly what I knew he was going to say anyway. His response undoubtedly piqued me. I envied these birds for their freedom, as compared to my own ensnared state. My father said we had enough; that I did not need to worry about a thing. In fact, we had enough to feed the entire city, all our lives.

But I could not justify this in my heart. I could not quell my feelings. They were real...for me. I was giving those birds what was already available to me. It was readymade; I wasn't creating anything special of my own. In reality, I had no idea what I could possibly do. There was so much here that I wondered if there was any space left for me to do anything new here.'

'Do you still feel that way?' Hyder asked, in the same way I confronted myself in the mirror every day in trepidation.

'I do. Every single minute of my life. It smothers me. I feel incomplete,' I responded, expressing my woe.

Hyder said nothing. He kept playing with the birds and enjoying their company. They too, seemed to love sitting on his shoulders, arms and head. I was deeply happy to have met him; this young man. It was inspiring to see the blend of innocence and wisdom in him. I was already beginning to cherish his friendship. He seemed to have nothing, yet he was totally free. Just like those birds.

'Often the places we choose to go to are places where we know we will get something,' he finally said. 'But you see, for us to get something, someone or something must offer it to us in the first place. We go to the places we consider sacred because we believe we will be heard there; that we will find what we seek. In reality, what we get is the courage and faith to move on in the journey that you are already on. Life itself is a sacred task, isn't it?'

Hyder went on speaking in a calm steady voice that was both soothing and healing to my pensive mind.

'Do you think these birds come here to stay, Musa? They merely know they will be fed here. So they come every day. But they do not stay longer because they know they will get what they are looking for. They eat their fill and then go on with their journeys, accomplish their tasks, feed their children, and make love. When they need to be fed, they know this place is available to them.

Just like *Allah* is available to us anywhere. It is not necessary to stay here. We must go on with our journeys. We are here to be on our own. Let God rest too. Free Him from deciding for us. Let us have the courage, like the oar that rows our boat. It pushes the water behind to go forward, knowing that the water, the lake, and the palace, will always be here.'

CHAPTER 18

Musa's Tales

I was grateful for Hyder's endearing presence. It is rare to meet someone and immediately know that he has come as an answer from the Universe.

'It must have been so enchanting to see this palace being built, with so many architects, designers, craftsmen and artisans at work, all creating this with their own hands!' Hyder exclaimed, admiring the entrance.

An opal *kamaan*, surrounded with colourful gems, was embedded in the grand door. It looked kingly and imperial indeed. A limestone pathway led from the palace to the lake. Large windows with gilt frames shone unblemished, as if the palace had been recently built. The rococo interiors, the high ceilings with massive chandeliers with their warm orange light, were mesmerising in their beauty. Golden tassels held back velvet curtains from the arched windows. The upholstery design of a goldfinch sitting on a bright orange flowering tree with green twigs, could not be estranged from the place. The *hamams* were a true delight with their mosaic baths. Indeed, it was a very royal palace!

'Each little stone, every chiselled crystal, every piece of mosaic and every pillar here represents the love and passion of the artisans who worked on them. It was built almost a century ago by my ancestors.'

We spent hours touring the magnificent place. Hyder was speechlessly observant for most of the time. He would mumble something in adoration every now and then, and continue his wide-eyed exploration. I was struck by his wonderment and the sheer humility and largeness of his heart. He had this infinite ability to appreciate the littlest of things.

'Hyder, I would like you to stay here as long as you want,' I said to him, overjoyed by his joy. 'In your company, I might perhaps find my answers to life.'

Hyder looked at me and smiled. 'Musa, don't you see that I too, am looking for the same thing – answers about life? I too, am incomplete. But thank you Musa, for asking me to stay. Your faith in finding your answer in me, who is himself still incomplete, gives me the confidence to move on; to journey on further. Musa, this palace is not only the most picturesque and sumptuous place I have ever seen, but it is truly perfect. So perfect that while I can cherish its beauty, I cannot add anything to it. I cannot bring more life to its ceilings or walls, or windows or doors. It has its own life and beauty, presence and existence. Being so perfect, it will not allow me to grow or see my purpose in life; that which I am looking for. The only place I can find my answers is in the world out there. Inside here is too beautiful. Outside, in all those incomplete things, I will find my purpose.'

Hyder spoke in a steady soothing voice, voicing his conviction that he must journey on. No words of mine would stop him from continuing on his path.

'Hyder my friend, that is exactly what I meant too,' I said to him. 'I am the only son and heir of a king. And I will be the only one to take this legacy forward. I have inherited this perfection. I know that this is written in my fate and no one can change that. But it makes me restless that I know my life too well, to know that my life is so bounded. It would be history repeating itself. But this is not the answer to my restlessness, the questions surging within my heart. I too, need to go out there, to see the world and find a corner where I am needed. Here, it is already too full.'

Looking down from an arched casement, Hyder gazed at the pigeons below. They came flocking in, ate the grain and flew off again, sometimes together, sometimes alone.

'Hyder, I believe you arrived in my life so I could leave the life I have here. I would like to join you in your journey. Will you accept me?' I prayed that he would, even knowing he was on his own *chilla*. Deep down, I desperately needed him to say 'yes', to make headway towards my own calling.

Hyder looked at me, smiled and hugged me. His hug was an embrace.

'Of course!' he said without hesitation. 'We shall be co-travellers!'

PART III

CHAPTER 19

365 Days of a Sufi

Month Four

I had no idea that my father had been a traveller, a seeker; that he had been a mystic himself. I knew him as a curious and pious soul, but I was humbled to hear his story from Musa. I now understood his gallant efforts during this intense phase of his life; it was both valiant and evolutionary. It became all the more important to me to know this side of his life.

Perhaps, amidst those stories, lay hidden the treasure I was seeking, the treasure that my father said his friend Musa had. I now realized that I had had another treasure with me all my life, in him, yet had never recognized it. I was also curious to know where these two friends went when they left the palace. Where did life take them? What inner compass did they follow? And why, in spite of his inheritance, was Musa now dressed in rags, dwelling on the street?

'Rashid,' Musa uttered my name, halting the train of my thoughts. We were still sitting by the lake, facing Musa's magnificent inheritance. 'I have brought you an inch closer to the treasure,' he said. 'Take it forward from here.'

Did that mean, I was to leave Musa alone? Was this all he had to share? My anxious thoughts leapt from one corner to another like a scurrying rat with nowhere to go.

'Musa, I really want to know what happened next,' I urged, unable to accept the idea that this might be all. I wasn't ready to leave yet.

But Musa insisted. 'Sometimes, the only way to know what happened next is to walk the path and experience it for yourself.'

'I agree, but I need a guide. I am still unripe,' my ingenuous heart broke into tears, to my surprise.

He smiled at my childlike persistence. 'You are like me when I first met your father – gullible, yet prudent. I wanted him to be with me, answer all my questions, and fill the empty spaces within me. I didn't know whether I wanted to understand the void or merely wanted to have something or somebody fill it for me. Well then, I will guide you up to a point. Then the rest of it, you must figure out yourself.'

I agreed. It was there, sitting beside that serene lake in the magnificent city of Pena, that I had a vague image of myself embarking on a journey alone. It was then that I had made up my mind to turn that vision into reality someday.

Musa's Tales

The next morning, your father and I went towards a mountain. We walked a long time along the city's main roads and through the rusty streets of old Pena. I had never seen my own world so closely until then. There were so many narrow lanes and by-lanes, filthy unpaved streets, with countless cramped houses. Some looked quaint, and some ramshackle. There were so many people, living and working so close together. There were so many sounds and smells. The hustle and bustle buzzed in my ears and I could barely hear Hyder's voice. But he did not seem to mind the surroundings. He was used to it perhaps, or he had somehow found a way to maintain his composure amidst all the chaos.

I just followed him, my heart unresisting, which surprised me too. All these years, I had lived a life of affluence, under the royal roof. All my needs had been instantly met. Many lands and houses were bought in my name in different parts of the world. The lake and the birds, the sounds and fragrances, were my constant companions. There was such peace, such silence. I was materially carefree.

So, being suddenly confronted with this strange unkempt world should have dismantled me. Yet there I was, following this young man, whom I had met just a few hours ago. Surely

I could keep the fire burning within me until we crossed this mess.

And soon the fire was to be put to test, when we came across a tiny rickety tea-stall, sitting in a narrow crowded alley. Needless to say, the place was swarming with people and chatter, and the smell of tea hung in the air. I was nauseous immediately. I felt rather claustrophobic. Everything seemed bedraggled. While Hyder was happy to pick up two clay cups of tea from the vendor's soiled hands, the elite in me was frantically jumping out to scream in denial.

This was a shocking experience for me. A table and a few chairs were the only furniture the tea-stall boasted, the other paraphernalia consisted of a hissing and blackened stove, an aluminium tea pot, into which was inserted a muslin straining cloth, brown with repeated use, and several translucent half-glasses and a few sun-baked clay cups. When Hyder offered me one of these, I looked at him, wondering how I could skip this. How could I possibly sip from a cup that had already been sipped by who knows how many people that day? I was not at all used to this. It was an alien world. I accepted the cup but the grim expression on my face certainly betrayed my inner disgust.

'Watch out, it's hot!' Hyder cautioned, an amused smile on his lips and in his eyes.

I held the cup with unwilling fingers, trying not to look into it, afraid to find scum floating on the surface. In wonder, I watched Hyder and many others relish the steaming brew. I was reluctant to take the plunge. I was absorbed in my own misgivings, drunk on the resistance that kept me far from being present in the moment.

Hyder drank the last of his tea and put the empty cup down on the table. It was the first time I saw such contentment on his face. He said with a kind smile, 'My friend, it isn't just about you having tea from a cup millions had drunk from. It is also about the tea, which has been consumed by many and made each one of us feel different. It is not the cup or the place that makes the tea different. It is the tea itself. It is not what you wear on the outside but what you are living inside you.'

Right then, his words were jewels to me. They brought me an inch closer to the truth, while giving me confidence about my decision to leave home. I listened carefully to what he said, feeling less disturbed about my immutable routine living in the palace. Looking back at it now, I see that I had become quite blasé in that kingly setting.

'I have always felt that God is overused – again and again by millions, in a trillion different ways. What if one day God shows up in front of you Musa, and you do not like his attire but you know it is Him? What would you do?'

With each word, I felt more and more grounded to my roots. My fingers had begun to finally grip the clay cup of tea, feeling its warmth. The aroma of spices was now bringing a tingling, refreshing sensation to my nostrils. My tea had gone from hot to warm as my thoughts became lucid and bearable.

Finally, I took a sip and said, 'Yes Hyder, I surely wouldn't want my tea to turn cold. I like it warm.' I sipped from the cup and smiled.

That tea was certainly special, for it was the tea that helped me lose my inhibitions. Its sweetness was beyond compare and held a love of its own. I like to think the tea too, was happy to be consumed by a loving, happy man rather than one driven to despair by his thoughts.

Meanwhile, Hyder ordered another tea to keep me company.

.

CHAPTER 21

Meru and Zaitoon had got accustomed to a routine – finishing their morning chores, cleaning the house, cooking together, and then taking a little short siesta before finally immersing themselves in reading *365 Days of a Sufi*. Every afternoon, Zaitoon would read aloud from her grandfather's journal and they would simply get lost in a reflective mode, imagining the characters and events.

'Do you think your grandfather was also a performing *chilla* when he wrote this book?' Meru asked, reflectively.

'Maybe,' Zaitoon replied. 'You think we are like Musa and Hyder?'

They couldn't wait to read more. Sometimes, the friends had great fun predicting what might happen next. They marvelled at how the wisdom in the stories was helping them see their own lives in a better and different light. To Meru, Ibne-Al-Rashid's life seemed similar to hers, while Zaitoon resonated with Musa's love for Hyder. Meru was so hooked to the stories that she could not thank her friend enough for reading them aloud to her.

Reading became such a gripping ritual in their everyday life that they would clean the space where they sat to read, burn incense and sage, and sometimes even light a candle to create a pure, enthralling ambience. They would complete their chores as quickly as they could so they would have more time to read.

One day, just as Zaitoon and Meru were about to begin their reading, they heard a loud crash outside. Alarmed, they sprinted up to the terrace in jitters, to see what had happened. The hoarding of the Children's Home had finally given up and come crashing down to the street below. The birds flapped away in alarm with that plummeting echo. Onlookers gathered around, gawking. Finally, two men simply picked up the fatigued signage and laid it to rest in a back alley.

Meru and Zaitoon noticed that the wall behind the hoarding had something encrypted on it, but the writing had faded over the years. Time and neglect had leached away its once vibrant life. Zaitoon tried to decipher the words, but could not.

Meru, in that moment, felt acutely handicap of not being able to read. With eyes luminous with unshed tears, she said, 'Zaitoon, I have realized I must learn to read and write. I only know how to weave. But I must design too. I must read the books I missed reading while growing up. Will you teach me?'

Zaitoon was pleased to hear this from her friend. 'Yes, I will. In return, will you teach me to weave?'

Meru laughed. 'Of course, I will!'

And just like Hyder and Musa, Meru and Zaitoon became co-travellers, excited to embark on the journey of learning.

$$\mathcal{L}$$

CHAPTER 22

365 Days of a Sufi

Month Five

Bismillah!

You can always teach what you know and you can always be open to learning something new. Teaching is an integral part of our lives. Sometimes, we teach without teaching, and we also learn without being taught. We humans have an integral ability to learn lessons from life and teaching about life to others. Our life is itself a lesson and a teacher.

Some people never get a chance to go to school, or learn a new language, but they never forget how to communicate with Allah. We all know that language, for it is embedded within us. So, at the core, we are all wise people. The real question is what we choose to do with that wisdom, and how often do we want to listen to what it says.

Ibne-Al-Rashid, November 1899

o

One day, one of my aunts had come home for a visit, to spend an evening with us over a cup of tea. She lived in a village not too far away but was visiting us after a long time. The seven of us, my brothers and sisters, sat encircling her, happy to hear the interesting stories of her life in the village and the students in her school. She was a teacher of languages. She taught Urdu and English. She loved music, dancing and reading, and often read to us some of her favourite poetry collections.

She brought many gifts for us that evening. So she opened her bag and one by one called each of us and handed us beautiful things. The gifts were bestowed with colourful floral and geometrically designed wrappers. Everyone got something wonderful – apparel, games, toys, dolls, stationery, sweetmeats. But when my turn came, she just gave me loose sheets of papers from old exercise books. They were papers that had remained unused at the end of the school year, which children tore out to reuse as rough papers. I was exasperated and hurt. I was so displeased in that moment, wondering why she had given me plain papers. That really upset me. It took away all my excitement.

Soon after she left, I started to cry, gazing out of the window and feeling lonely despite the whole busy world around me. Several days passed, but I couldn't overcome the hurt of not being valued. I felt abandoned and worthless. The memory of it vexed me every single day. That first night, I remember that I didn't even pray. I tossed and turned in my bed, between my siblings, feeling they were more special and precious than me. Maybe there was something wrong with me, I thought. I simply did not understand.

Finally, one evening, she visited us again for a festive supper. My guard was up. I reproached her with my silence. Nor did I look into her eyes. Instead of joining in for supper with the others, I just sat in the balcony, quietly looking at the formation of vagrant clouds. But, a few minutes later, she came and sat down next to me. Placing her hand on my shoulder she asked, 'So Rashid, have you started writing?'

Suddenly, my anger dissipated. The gift I wanted was already within me, and she knew much more about my skills than I did. I finally realized what I was supposed to do with those pieces of paper. She told me that the children in her school had willingly given her the remaining pages in their books when she told them about me. And as I looked at her, feeling a little sorry for my silliness, she produced a beautiful diary from her bag and handed it to me. It had a seaweed green cover, with golden archaic designs on it. A silken bookmark rested between the pages. It looked simple but the symbols made it distinctly classic.

'Those papers were for you to begin your writing. This one is for continuation when you know the story you want to tell,' she said, smiling at me. Her eyes radiated trust, genuine love and concern.

My eyes welled up as I stood up and hugged her tight. I told her how sorry I was for my behaviour.

Then she said something I'll never forget: 'I am indeed a teacher of languages, but I understand silence too.'

That is when I began to realize that every experience of disappointment is actually a turning point in our lives, either to begin living our dreams or to remind us to continue living. I decided to preserve the diary until I was ready to actually put down the words that came from the vales of my soul.

This diary is thus a reminder for me; a memorable epitaph of my life.

CHAPTER 23

When they were done reading that evening, Zaitoon gently shut the book. She slowly slid her fingers over its golden borders and stroked the tail of its silken bookmark. It had drizzled that day and the earthy aroma of freshly watered earth was in the air.

'Can you imagine Meru, this is the same diary my grandfather's aunt gifted him? I am amazed at how those empty pages are now filled with immortal stories of life. Is it not inspiring? Imagine if he had never written them! I would never have known about my ancestors. This must have been so precious to him,' Zaitoon said.

'As it is to us now,' Meru said reflectively, thinking how there existed no such history of her own ancestors. Yet, looking at the golden bordered diary, Meru understood that though her life at the moment looked much like loose sheets of paper, they would one day be bound together, and it was she who would write her own story on those pages. This thought stiffened her determination to learn to read and write. It was the first time Meru had made a conscious choice, using the freedom she had.

On the other hand, Zaitoon seemed to be sure that her grandfather's diary had come to her at the right time, when life itself felt open to be redefined, preparing her to weave it into a beautiful design. She found herself worrying less about *Ammi*. Instead, she found a way to channel her anxieties by spending positive time with her friend and accepting the fact that Meru's presence in her life gave her strength and resilience.

In this way, the two precocious friends arrived at a point where each one was ready to move past their limiting thoughts and personal worries.

That evening, they sat beside *Ammi* on the *charpoy*, watching the drizzle. The sooty clouds overhead had finally decided to release their own long-held burdens. Though cold and chilly, the light rain brought with it a tinge of warmth and the hope of a sunny day the next morning.

CHAPTER 24

Musa's Tales

Moving on from the tea-stall, Hyder and I continued our journey. We walked for hours and hours, gallivanting along the streets, lanes, parks, markets and the forest, until we finally made our sunset abode on a cliff. This was the first time I was going to sleep on the ground, in a windswept place under the open sky. I wondered if seeking freedom really required you to walk through crowded lanes and sleep on stones.

But I was with Hyder, and his ways always kept me inquisitive. He was happy to rest his back on the cliff. Folding his neck scarf under his head, he asked me if I was going to spend the entire night standing. To this, the answer was 'no', of course. I was tired by our long wearying day. So I let myself loose under the colourful stretches of the open sky. A deep sigh left my space as I slumped against my little valise. How beautiful it was to let go of all my resistance and comforts and to feel the divinity of the stars, shining down to greet me!

Deep silence took over as the last stretch of amber light and a streak of mauve willingly surrendered to the horizon.

'It isn't about letting go of those comforts Musa; it is about coming out of our habits,' Hyder posited. 'Sometimes, when we don't get a chance to experience something, it's not because we don't mean to experience them. But it is when you travel that you realize what else is possible. It isn't about comparing the miseries of your past with the experience you are having now. It's only about letting go and travelling, telling the wanderer inside you that it is also okay to return. You do not have to fight with what you are leaving to travel to where you are going. And where you are going, you might not even stay there for long, you may even go further.

So a traveller is someone who knows that he has the choice to take yet another turn and also has a *point of return*. Sometimes, our way back home is also a journey in itself. One comes to that point too while travelling I believe, Musa. But you travel back as a different person, seeing the same thing from the different light inside you.'

Hyder seemed to have understood my edgy feelings and occluded mind. Indeed, I was at the edge of an abyss of the unknown. The only known at that point for me was my deep connection with Hyder, and my faith in his infallible words; nothing else. His presence was my console.

Under that sky I stopped struggling; stopped fighting; stopped feeling that I had to leave all my comforts in order to feel my freedom. That night, before my eyelids drooped in sleep, I told myself that I was ready for this journey. I was ready to travel to those spaces and places, to sip that cup of tea, in which millions had found respite.

CHAPTER 25

Month Six

One day, I was cleaning the windows of my house. Loneliness was beginning to follow my every breath. It was not easy to live alone. I had my down days. While I washed the muck off the glass panes, I saw a woman carrying a basket of vegetables on her head, calling out to people that they were freshly plucked from her own garden. As she walked with her head held high, she looked elegant to me. She seemed to be in her early thirties. She had on some make-up and wore a string of pearl necklace and a gold bracelet. There was also a little puppy that tagged along behind her. I wondered what a sophisticated woman like her was doing selling vegetables?

She saw me at the window and stopped. 'Would you like to buy some fresh vegetables, Sir? They are from my wonderful garden. I grow them. You would not have any complaints.'

I could not hide my astonishment and asked politely, 'Don't mind my asking, but what makes you come out and roam the streets selling vegetables? You seem from a good family. Pardon my judgement and curiosity.'

She seemed amused. Glancing from the window to the cleaning cloth in my hand, she said, 'The same thing that got you to cleaning the window!'

I gave a sigh and nodded. Pointing to her basket, I bought some mixed-breed tomatoes and some strong chillies from her. As promised, they were the best. In return, she told me her story.

That night, as I laid my head on my pillow, my eyes wandered to the dark sky through the open window by my bed. The sky looked alone too, just like me, just like the woman. She had become a widow early in life, and now lived with the memories of her years with her husband. Together, they had planted many vegetables and fruits in their garden, and tended to them lovingly. Now, the house was surrounded by trees bearing all kinds of fruits and a garden full of vegetables. When her husband died, she had wanted to give up. The little garden-farm remained untended for a long time. But it did not die. The plants continued to bloom and bear fruit, as if to tell her that the love she had shared with her husband still lived. They reminded her to breathe, to push her way back to life. And in her attempt to talk to other humans, to come out of her loneliness, she started to sell the vegetables. It helped her to resume contact with the world. Each morning, she dressed to feel her own presence in her skin, and set out on her journey of getting back to life.

$$\text{\textcurrency}$$

CHAPTER 26

365 Days of a Sufi

Month Seven

One day a young boy innocently asked his mother, 'What is the heart of a *Sufi* like?'

The mother said to her son, 'Once upon a time there was a pet lover. He had a little sparrow that he served and loved for many years. One day, he had to go away for a few days to another city, so he asked his little son to take care of the sparrow until he returned. A few days later, when the man returned, he was surprised to find the cage empty. When he asked his son about the little sparrow, the son said that he had opened the cage and let it fly away. The man was furious. He had taken care of the sparrow for years and now his son had let it go? 'But that is my way of taking care,' he said to his father. 'To free it.'

'What is the heart of a *Sufi* like?' the son had asked and this was the best way his mother could explain it. Both father and son cared for the sparrow in their own way. They loved in their unique ways. Neither of them was incorrect. They both represented the heart of a *Sufi*. For one, it was about *keeping* what is loved, and for the other it was about *freeing* what is loved.

'A *Sufi*'s heart is like that, my son,' said the mother. 'A

Sufi wants to free his heart, yet keep his love for the Beloved within its boundaries. A *Sufi*'s heart also frees the Beloved from the confines of his heart, to find it in everyone.'

The mother continued, 'But the story doesn't end there, my son. Two days later, the sparrow returned, sitting on the window sill and chirping. Both father and son were overjoyed to see it return. The father understood that the lover knows his way back home. He understood that the sparrow did not need a cage. It knew it was loved by him and that was enough. The sparrow was free. He was free. The sparrow was love. He was love. Both father and son got what they wanted – a free-spirited sparrow. A *Sufi* knows he needs to give himself the freedom to love and that he needs to love the wings of freedom. A *Sufi* knows that God knows his home and it has no doors.'

The son looked at his mother and smiled, his heart content.

$$\mathcal{C}$$

CHAPTER 27

Musa's Tales

When dawn broke, I woke to find Hyder was missing. My heart skipped a beat. I looked around anxiously but the fog limited the scope of my vision. Even the silhouette of the surrounding mountains that I had seen last evening, was out of sight. Suddenly, I realized how cold and silent the place was.

I waited for some time, but then restlessness got the better of me. Panicking, I began to search for Hyder again. A few minutes later, I caught sight of him, sitting on a large rock. A deep sigh released itself from my heart. Anxiety liberated itself from my nerves and I went and sat near him.

'Hyder, you scared me!' I complained.

He merely smiled, looking into my eyes. His own eyes shone bright and he seemed relaxed. He turned his gaze to a distant space, where my eyes turned too. One could only see clouds and heavy fog.

'Hyder,' I muttered, curious to know what he was looking at, 'what's on your mind?'

There was a long pause, then he said without looking away, 'We will not be here tomorrow morning, Musa, so I am listening.'

'Listening?'

'Yes. The song of the morning! Can you hear the little trills and chirping of the birds; their melody?'

I strained my ears to hear. 'Yes, they are pretty loud. I can hear them,' I said.

'So keep listening,' he suggested.

I went to sit on another rock nearby and turned my gaze towards the clouds. I listened intently to the song of the morning – the chirping of the birds in distinct synchronicity. My anxiety abated and my mind shifted from unpleasant thoughts to silence.

Hyder was as still as the rock on which he sat. But he said quietly, 'I've heard that mornings in the mountain are mesmerising. My Master told me that wherever I travelled, to whichever part of the world, and however tired I was, however fulfilled or miserable, whatever my state, I should never miss the mornings. Look at those clouds. They are moving, moving apart. Look at the mist. It is slowly disappearing.'

My eyes attempted to reach to the moving clouds yonder. They were swiftly on their way to somewhere, their soft edges losing themselves in some invisible world. Birds cooed.

'In a few moments Musa, you will know why my Master asked me never to miss the mornings.'

As the clouds gradually separated with each passing moment, they unveiled a truly marvellous sight to behold – a range of snow-capped mountains. Some high, some small, some jagged, others merging together as if they had adopted each other. It was a family of peaks, standing tall and proud, guarding the morning with their grandeur. The sky bowed over them. What a sight those fresh sun-bleached snow caps standing quietly were. Breathing in the pure crisp morning air, my heart was suddenly uplifted

'Hyder, you were right,' I finally said. 'I thank you, my friend, for bringing me here.'

'And I thank you Musa, for crossing my path here.' Hyder had a mystical smile on his face as he said these words.

By the time my heart had begun settling into the valleys between those mountains and my eyes had stopped scanning the scarlet horizon, Hyder was ready to resume his journey.

CHAPTER 28

365 Days of a Sufi

My aunt had shared her favourite story with all of us seven siblings. How I cherished the time spent sitting together, listening to her intently. She was a gifted storyteller; a true teacher. She had heard the story from her grandmother, who had in turn heard it from her grandmother. Now I share it here with you. And someday you will continue the legacy by sharing it with others. Interesting, right? Stories are inheritance. Perhaps stories are the only inheritance that grows when they are shared with others.

This story is called: *Miracle in the Desert of Minaara.*

The land was barren, and so was Hazrat's heart. The sun was at its zenith and Hazrat could keep his eyes open no more. Sweat rolled off his body. The fiery desert was like a roaring lion – a rich gold, with not a drop of water in sight. But Hazrat refused to give into to his weariness. He lumbered on with sagging shoulders, affirming his mind that he must continue a little further, so that he could find the miracle. He walked up and down the sand dunes in the lonely desert underneath the wild sky.

Hazrat was a young boy with a curious mind. His quest was to know if miracles truly exist, and if so, to whom did they happen? He had heard from many that those who walked the desert of Minaara alone, found the answer. The desert belonged to everyone, old, young, children, poor, rich, married, widowed… everybody. The desert was known to speak to all. It knew languages of all the ages. It had its unique way of communicating with everyone.

Hazrat had walked far from his home. His shadow began to fade as the sun was about to set. He turned to look back. All he could see were his tiny footprints on the sand. *Hmm… good. I'm sure these footprints will serve as a map to take me back home.* With the glow of a smile on his dry lips, he walked on. So many questions engulfed his jarred mind: *What if the sand was not able to imprint footsteps? What if shadows never formed? What if the sun never rose? Perhaps I would not then be able to make my way home. And I would be lonely without my shadow.*

Soon, the sun slipped into the sand and stars began to twinkle in the sky. The night was luminous. The moon was bright, as though it wished to make merry with little Hazrat. He felt a tinge of moistness in the air. He could smell the intoxicating fragrance of wet sand. *There must indeed be a small pond nearby*, he thought.

Hazrat walked faster, and finally jumped over a sandy mound to come upon a quiet placid pond. He opened his arms wide, pulled his bag off his shoulders, and lost no time in jumping into the water. The water was chill. He bathed and quenched his thirst. Hazrat played joyously, splashing the water over himself.

Finally, he got out and sat on the cold soft sand. Looking at the moonlit pond, he thought about this wonderful creation of God. Hazrat opened his bag to get out some food, but it had a rancid smell. He looked around to see if he could find anything to eat. His eyes fell on some date trees. He ran to one and picked what he could.

Hazrat then lay down on the cool sand, using his bag as a pillow. Looking up at the blanket of shining stars, he munched the sweet dates one by one, thinking about his quest. *What are miracles after all? Who can give them to me?* As his tired eyes closed in sleep, he murmured his regular prayer, thanking God for the day, then said, 'Tomorrow, I hope I find a miracle'.

Morning blossomed. The sun was much brighter and friendlier than the previous day. Hazrat filled his bottle with water and moved on once again, into the dreary desert. He was hungry. The dates weren't enough to fill his stomach. *Oh, I'm extremely hungry, God. Where do I find something to eat now?* he wondered. Hazrat reminisced about how his loving mother would feed him. Today, he was missing every morsel. Hazrat's eyes filled with tears.

At some distance, he saw a small tent. He could see some clothes hanging on a rope, and someone sitting. He walked in that direction, hoping to find someone who would fill his hungry stomach. As he came closer, he saw an old woman stirring something in a clay pot over a fire.

The boy's shadow reached the old lady. She looked up, gazed at the boy, and smiled. Her eyes had a friendly look. In a sweet, sonorous voice, she said, 'Come, come, sit here. You must be hungry.' She cleaned an area with a piece of cloth and made space for Hazrat to sit comfortably.

He was astonished; it seemed like the kind lady had been expecting him! Unclasping his bag, he sat down. She reminded him of his grandmother, who always knew what he wanted. He remembered her caring hands on his head, pulling the blanket up around him at night.

The lady quickly prepared two bowls of soup and two pieces of *bolani* with potatoes and asked Hazrat to eat. As they sat across from each other, the lady asked softly, 'Who are you, my child and why are you here?'

Hazrat was relishing the taste of the hot soup. Wiping his mouth with the back of his tanned hand, he answered, 'I am Hazrat, and I am here in search of *miracles.*' He continued to gulp down the soup merrily. 'I am in search of someone who can lend it to me so that I can share it with others. I have heard that whoever walks alone in this desert, finds it.'

The lady listened, her heart filled with affection for the boy. 'Hazrat, I live alone here,' she said. 'Every day I wish I had someone to talk to. I hoped for someone to share a meal I made with, with whom I could just spend some smiling moments. I knew that one day God would listen to my prayers. Today, when I saw you, my heart was filled with joy, feeling my prayer was answered in you. This, to me, is a *miracle.* You are a *miracle* for me.'

Hazrat saw the gleam of joy in the lady's eyes. Her delight was obvious. Her wrinkled face looked effulgent. Soon, he finished his soup, feeling energetic and ready to resume walking through the desert again. He thanked the lady for her kindness and humility.

As he was about to leave, the lady asked him to wait for a minute and ducked inside the dark cavern of the tent. After a few moments, she came out with a piece of gold in her hand. She said, 'Hazrat, this is a small gift for you. Remember this as a precious memento for making someone happy just by showing up. You gave me a chance to thank you.'

In that moment Hazrat looked at the lady in bewilderment. She looked ageless, full of wisdom; her face radiant and angelic. He did not know what he had done to deserve a gift from her. The old lady embraced him and bade him farewell.

'Wow, what a miracle!' Hazrat chuckled.

He walked for a few miles till the sun was setting again. It was time for him to stop. While he rested his head on the sand, he slipped out the little piece of gold from his pocket. The angelic face of the old lady flashed before his eyes. *Her heart was so pure,* he thought. Closing his eyes, Hazrat prayed for the lady. He remembered his parents, his friends, and his neighbours. Soon the night and slumber claimed him.

Hazrat woke to a pleasant day but his calf muscles were aching. He hobbled at every step. He was tired and prayed for help. As he lifted his head to drink some water, he saw a tall man standing at some distance, with a camel. The man was sturdy and broad-shouldered, and had strong hands. His sweaty head held a *keffiyeh,* and he wore a *thawb* draped over the shoulders and a neckerchief around his neck.

Even as Hazrat wondered about the man and his camel, the man approached him saying, 'Hey little boy, what are you doing here alone?'

Hazrat looked up at him as if he was looking up at the sky and said, 'I'm not alone Sir, you are with me.'

'Indeed yes, smart boy.'

The man and boy laughed together.

'Sir, I am Hazrat, and I came here in search of *miracles*. If I could find them, I could share them with the world. Now I am returning home.'

'So, did you succeed in finding *miracles*?' asked the man curiously.

'Yes, I did,' Hazrat said.

'That is wonderful. Perhaps, now I have too,' the man replied.

Hazrat looked perplexed and curious. 'Really? You too? How?'

'Come, sit on my camel and I will give you the answer. I will take you to your city if you want.' Hazrat was elated and thankful. He immediately remembered the words of the old lady: *You gave me a chance to thank you.* And now he, Hazrat, was thanking this man. *What could be more miraculous than this when I had no strength to walk?'* he thought as he clambered onto the kneeling camel's back.

'What could be more miraculous than this? I thought when I saw those tiny footprints,' said the man, directing Hazrat's gaze towards the small imprints in the sand. 'Hazrat, I was here to exchange my camel, with another trader. I lost my way. I was perplexed and in need of help, then I saw the little footprints. I followed them thinking they would lead me to the city. My wife and children would have worried if I did not reach home on time. I thanked God for showing me the way. Then I saw you and I was sure those footprints were yours. So I thank you, little one.'

Hazrat listened to the man silently.

'So I hope that by now you will have understood what you can do with the miracles in you,' the man said. 'You have shown me the way without knowing it yourself. I believe miracles are not only in the giving, but also in receiving, little one.'

'Just as I received your camel ride and you received my footprints?' asked Hazrat.

'Absolutely, little one,' the man affirmed.

Hazrat was certain that miracles were in him, within him. He knew that miracles were present in others too. His search was a miracle in itself. He slipped out the golden coin from his pocket and kissed it. He could see his footprints, the sweet date trees, and the cool pond. He was very happy. His quest was over, though not his journey.

He asked the man to halt the camel near the pond. In its clear still waters, he saw his own reflection. His eyes were twinkling, his face radiant and sparkling, just like that of the old lady and the camel man. Hazrat knew he too, had the spark. His questions had been finally answered.

The man and the boy merrily journeyed back home, one riding the camel, the other walking beside it. As they went they shared their stories with each other.

o

All seven brothers and sisters sat enraptured by the enthralling story. My aunt concluded with the words that have stayed with me all these years: 'I am sure even God was following their footprints. Do you want to join them too?

Join in the joy of miracles?'

She chuckled as we all nodded eagerly. In our imaginations we were in the distant desert, riding with the boy on the camel.

PART IV

CHAPTER 29

By now, Meru was quite familiar with the alphabet. And Zaitoon was making progress with the *zari* work. Each enjoyed teaching the other. Gulfam *Kaka* was happy to let Meru work from Otto, and with an extra pair of helping hands, she was able to produce double the stock she normally did. It was profitable for both. This gave Meru more time to teach Zaitoon as well. Occasionally, Zaitoon accompanied Meru to drop off the clothes and pick up the new lot. Meru also sought inspiration from the collections in the Otto bazaars.

Sakina *Khala* sometimes helped as well, passing the threads or segregating the colourful sequins. This allowed her to use her time in a constructive way. She loved being with the two girls, feeling secure and happy. She was improving day by day, making progress in her movements. Seeing this made Zaitoon contented and hopeful.

Life became not only more interesting, but fascinating as well, as the two friends helped each other selflessly. They bought alphabet books for Meru, and *zari* design books for Zaitoon. Meru was a fast learner. Despite never having been to school, she was skilled in Math. Her experience with counting and accounting at the *zari* shop also helped her. She was used to the daily mental math required at the shop – the length of cloth, the quantum of thread, and the number of work hours required to complete each piece of fabric. Calculation had been directly or indirectly a part of her daily life. But only at this juncture, teaching *zari* work to Zaitoon, did she see the threads of her past coming together to form a design.

Zaitoon was quite happy with Meru's simple yet precise teaching. *Zardosi, Minakari, Salma-Sitara*, all these terms fascinated Zaitoon. But best of all she loved the *kinari* work – the embroidery done at the edges and on tassels. She knew she was not nearly as efficient as Meru, but she tried her best to meet the goal for the day.

'A language is much easier to learn than an art form,' Zaitoon opined one day while Meru was taking it one day at a time to read aloud the sentences and comprehend them. 'Teaching comes naturally to you, Meru. I so enjoy being your student. Every day there is something new.'

Such a compliment coming from her learned friend, whom she considered to be far ahead of her, meant a great deal to Meru.

'You are an artist,' Zaitoon often commented.

Meru felt accepted and was grateful that life had offered her this chance to teach Zaitoon, whom she had come to love and respect a great deal by now. It was because of this wonderful exchange of skills that Meru had finally discovered this side of herself. She had begun to trust the course of her life ahead.

'I understand now that often we miss out on knowing ourselves just because we don't have the opportunity,' said Meru, handing a golden thread to Zaitoon. 'Here, use this one. And weave it gently into that leafy design along the edges.'

It made her happy to see how Zaitoon's fingers were now more assured and less hesitant. Their little teach-and-learn project took place on a mat spread on the terrace. It was on that mat that they came to meet their 'other' selves – the selves that had lain hidden and unexpressed within, all these years. They had left their innocent selves behind when they had parted as little girls, only to be reunited as responsible women.

And as they wove the golden threads in and out, Meru shared what her mind was beginning to see.

'You know Zaitoon, while teaching you I suddenly discovered the value of what I had considered to be mundane. My daily work that had helped me make money has become an assimilation of wisdom – that of art, skill, craft, creativity and colours. And beyond these, the connected stories. I am beginning to see the value in ordinary things too – how each artist weaves a different design, unique to their vision, using the same threads. I find myself going back to the basic questions – who invented these threads, the designs, the artwork? What might their origins be? Why these traditions?'

'But imagine what an opportunity it has become for both of us to create something unique and original,' said Zaitoon. 'Even for me Meru, the humdrum chores of the house no longer seem mundane. Every day is like a miracle. Perhaps I am exaggerating.'

'No, my friend, you are not,' Meru said it with calm confidence. 'We are here to learn, to invent, to discover.' Meru was amazed by her own change of attitude. She too, had begun to feel like an artist.

Both friends immersed themselves in gently weaving the unadorned corners of the scarf while *Ammi* rested on the *charpoy*, listening to their maturing exchanges.

CHAPTER 30

Meru and Zaitoon ventured out one evening to watch a musical play in town. It was part of the Annual Otto Festival and there was a feeling of gaiety all around. It was the first time Meru and Zaitoon had been out at night on the streets, now decorated with colourful lights and lanterns. This was a festival the city of Otto was known for. A tall pole stood in the middle of the parade ground with the name of the musical show on a silken banner dancing in the East Wind. The entire population seemed to have turned up to watch the performance. The audience was regaled with free refreshments and sweet drinks.

Though Zaitoon had visited fairs and the circus with her parents when she was little, it was all new to Meru. She had never seen a play performed in her entire life, let alone a musical one. So, being there that evening with her friend felt extremely thrilling. This time, freedom tasted sweet, very different from when she had first come to live with Zaitoon. She was now beginning to befriend this freedom rather than fear it. Now that she was here, she was greedy for more – *more knowledge, more dreams, more love!* Her life had turned around for good.

The musical drama was Zaida, an ambitious and enthusiastic young girl who yearned to pursue education and become a teacher in a school. But she belonged to a poor family, and lived in a ghetto. Her mother suffered from mental illness and her father, a carpenter, was the sole provider for the family. Zaida had four younger siblings – two brothers and two sisters – whom she looked after, though she was herself just a young girl who also needed to be cared for. She cooked, cleaned, washed clothes and utensils, and served food to her family. And when her mother's illness worsened, she went to work. Life was tough and the passion inside her found no space to bloom. Soon it shrivelled into a tiny corner of her heart. Zaida was overworked all the time, exhausted and weary. As the days passed, all her desires were doused and her dreams buried in the cemetery of time. She gave all she had to her family, receiving nothing but pain and sorrow. Melancholy was her companion, resting in her shadow.

One day, a fierce storm struck the city and took with it hundreds of homes; Zaida's among them. The walls fell and the roof flew into the wind. All the family's sparse belongings were gone. There was nowhere to go. As the rains continued to pour down, all they had left was the open sky. It was as if Zaida's pain had been laid bare, to be felt by the whole world; the entire city weeping.

Seeking shelter, Zaida and her family temporarily moved to the house of a distant relative, where they were well taken care of. There, she met a young man, Zaheer, the relative's son, who grew fond of her. But he was a crook; a rogue involved in smuggling drugs. Little did Zaida know what her vulnerability had exposed her to. Zaheer had no education, no serious work, and was known for his addiction. Even so, Zaida could not resist accepting the little care and affection he offered, the only love she had ever received in her hard life. One day, unbeknownst to their families, the two absconded and got married.

When the play ended, the thespian-narrator told the audience that the play was based on a true story. Though simple, the story was one of human tribulation, of fate. He spoke at length about love, saying in a stentorian voice, 'To love or not to love is one of those major decisions that changes the course of one's life, for the better or for worse. And we all face this decision at least once in our lives.'

He went on to discuss the story further, speaking about how the lack of love can make anyone susceptible to anything that remotely resembles it. In the play, the girl becomes a silent escapist owing to the frustration she bears within her. To her, Zaheer seemed like a solution to the drudgery of her loveless life. What might have happened next in the story was left to the audience to decide. The narrator simply underlined the fact that love and care are necessary to live a good life. Basic human nature seeks it.

And so, mesmerised by the performances and the tale, Zaitoon and Meru walked home that night, speaking of love. For the first time, Meru considered her experience of love, simple and plain. She had loved her parents, Gulfam *Kaka,* and the *zari* work she did. But now that she was on her own, exploring life, she realized that life was not limited to just loving what was within our own walls; that there exists more love within us for loving the world beyond these boundaries.

The two friends recognized that there were certainly those who had suffered, who needed love and were perhaps anxiously waiting for some magic to turn their lives around. The perilous plight of the girl in the play filled their hearts with empathy and compassion. Though they were minuscule beings, they felt they were also important parts of the larger world.

'You know Zaitoon, I do not know what I might have succumbed to by now, if I had remained alone in my house in Bashirbagh.'

Zaitoon gave Meru a quick hug. 'I feel the same,' she said softly.

The musical play had compelled the two friends to reflect on their own stories. They had found refuge in each other and now their warm hearts were ready to reach out to the beautiful stars that gleamed in the sky. And as they trudged back home that night, a chord of love was struck. Love for the whole world.

$\mathcal{S}$

CHAPTER 31

The next morning the sky was filled with rainbow colours. With cherry and purple stretches across the horizon and a crispy wind whistling in the presence of a new day, Meru stood on the terrace, once again bewitched by the view. She caught a whiff of rosy fragrance from the pots nearby. Pellets of dew drops rested on the smooth pink petals. It made her feel that a special time was about to begin in her life.

As the birds chirped and the sun spread its warmth before showing its face, Meru's heart felt like celebrating life with gusto. As she stretched, her eyes fell on the terrace of the Children's Home. It looked lifeless and empty...forlorn. But just then, her eyes caught sight of a soft white feather floating in mid-air, and she got herself back to the zeal of the day. A new fire had been ignited within her and now she began to actively think about what to do next in life. It was evident to both Meru and Zaitoon that they had been re-united for a purpose; that a new life was about to start in some way.

'Meru, is it okay if we read now, instead of this evening? Zaitoon suggested, coming out onto the terrace.

'I am always ready for that,' Meru answered.

'I have to take *Ammi* to the *hakim* this evening. So I thought we could catch up with our reading earlier.'

'Of course, but first come and look at the sky! I've never seen such a beautiful sunrise. Where I lived, the children were always enthusiastic about the days. No matter what, their playful voices would be the first to sing and start chattering in rhythm, even before the birds began to flutter their feathers and chirp. This morning somehow inspires me towards the exceptional. But look, there's no one on the terrace of the Home. Isn't that strange? There are so many children there yet no one ever seems interested in the beautiful sunrises or play in such a spacious terrace.'

Even when Meru had arrived here for the first time and her own wounds were deeply lacerated, her concern for the Children's Home had been real. She was often drawn towards it.

'You are right, Meru,' Zaitoon replied, looking over the parapet. 'The place seems utterly devoid of joy. I wonder what life must be like inside those walls.'

Meru and Zaitoon stood watching the decrepit structure, a silent, unhappy presence cast against the bright morning sky.

$$\mathscr{F}$$

CHAPTER 32

Month Eight

I woke one day to the sound of a bird. It was a new trill, and strangely loud.

Every day was a new discovery, living alone. I would generally wake up early every morning, sit up in my bed, pick up my *tasbih,* and then fall into a deep state in the remembrance of *Allah*, turning the little beads over and over. Sometimes, I fell asleep, and many a time memories would take me back to another time. Then I would wake with a jolt, laughing at my own infantile mind.

However, that morning was different. The bird would not stop tweeting outside my window. It had a kind of ear-piercing trill. Perhaps it was fortunate for I woke up and looked outside. It was dark and a deep blue hue spread everywhere. A hill overlooked my little home. People said the hill was actually the first meteor to fall on this planet. Atop it was a small *community space* where people flocked for *sama* gatherings, for silent *zikr*, and for rest. I had always wanted to go up there someday. However, I was so engrossed in my own aloneness and settling in that I did not feel like leaving home. I realized that this temporary home where I had lodged to spend my last days, had unknowingly become my place of escape.

Meanwhile, the chirping got louder, so I walked to the window to take a closer look. The bird sat on the elm tree outside my window. It was as little as my index finger. Its sound though, was far from small. It had blue-green feathers layered closely on each other, and a long beak that did not look suitable for its small body. I had never seen that bird before. As my glance steadied on it, suddenly it paused. A strange silence filled the air as we gauged each other. A few minutes later, it started to sing again, this time at a much lower volume. To my surprise, it flew straight to me and sat on the window sill. It kept looking at me with its charcoal black eyes, which didn't quite seem to fit its face either. It seemed fearless about my close proximity to it.

I had sensed by now that the bird had something to tell me. My unlikely guest had captivated me with its piercing glance and intense voice. Soon, I felt my focus zooming into its eyes, and zoning out of everything else around me. And when it blinked, I felt as if all of humanity had moved, as if I had lived a lifetime – my past, present and future – within that split second. In no time, it was swiftly flying in the direction of the mountain, right to the top.

I was intrigued by this experience, and the fact that I could see the bird clearly, flying to the mountain to perch atop the roof of the community space, even though it was so tiny. Its little wings shone, even at that distance. And as I stared at it, I had a moment of clarity. The appearance of the bird that morning was a sign. Rather, it was an omen – a calling to step out of this house and go to the mountain, for my aloneness had become my comfort. Even if one finds *Allah* inside oneself, one should not sit with it for too long. It is good to take *Allah* for a stroll in the garden made by the benevolent Almighty Himself.

And as this realization dawned on me, I found the bird was no longer visible. I had lost sight of it. I searched for it but everything on the mountain looked as tiny as a little ant. It was a moment of pure wonderment for me. The message came strangely and strongly – that I wasn't just meant to sit alone at home, but to travel up the mountain.

So began my journey.

$$\mathcal{L}$$

CHAPTER 33

It had already been over a month since I had joined Hyder. He was a man of stupendous courage and deep wisdom, and I was troubled by my own lack of both. I was still anxious about walking so far, to unknown places, about what I was doing with my life.

One day, I asked him where we were going next. He looked at me and said, 'Nowhere. Are we really going anywhere, anyway?' His answer frightened me and plunged deeper into my dilemma. I didn't know how to react. Going back to the palace was certainly a big no, but walking endlessly towards an unknown destination made me feel equally apprehensive.

We kept walking. It was hot. We had by now reached another city, with magnificent architectural structures, monuments and statues. Words of Holy Scripture were inscribed on the walls of local buildings and public places. We entered a large museum. It was colossal, its ceilings as high as the sky. It was a colourful structure with artistic carvings on the doors, panels and façades. On the walls next to the large windows, hung intricately woven tapestries.

Although it resembled my own palace, this one seemed to captivate and enchant in its own way. It was so colourful and finely sculpted that it charmed me. It was my turn to be lost in admiration, just as Hyder had been when he visited our palace in Pena. I wondered how many artisans, architects, stonemasons and labourers must have worked together to create such exquisite beauty!

The museum was filled with throngs of people gazing at the artefacts and ornaments, archery equipment and draperies used in the olden days. It also showcased the life of the architect-founder who had designed the museum. There were pictures from his childhood, boyhood, youth... till his death. Yes, the founder of this place was himself a renowned architect – Mahmut Abdullah. Time had elapsed certainly, but his work had lost none of its lustre. It remained beautiful, grand and immortal. Hundreds of visitors came every day, only to be filled with awe and wonderment at his creation and collections.

We went in with a scholarly guide, who told us the history of everything housed in the numerous sections of the museum. Everything had a unique story. There was a separate section that displayed the architect's belongings – paintings, clothes and other personal items such as his tools, his journal made of canvas sheets, some of his writings, pencils, and so many other little things. A huge effigy of him stood in a glass wall.

'He was an artist,' the guide told us as we walked along a long cloister, overlooking lawns and porches, to a semi-circular cupola in a turret, which offered an enviable view.

'But before all this happened, he was just a common man who went broke in business,' the guide said, smiling at our surprise. 'He lived with his wife in Kewa, a small village about 6500 kilometres from here. Kewa no longer exists on the map today, except as a piece of history in the hearts of people. Mahmut Abdullah was aggrieved and furious with the supercilious God who had brought him so low. His heart was filled with bitterness over the loss of his business.

One day, exhausted by his own irate temper, he said to his wife that he was tired of being patient and that he had suffered enough, that he did not deserve such a life of struggle. He felt that his art received no recognition in this world. There was no one knocking on the door but the army of failure. No sutures could bind his endless wounds. He described to his wife how each night he dreamt that someone was knocking on the door. When he opened it, there was a soldier whose face could not be seen. He wore a suit of armour that covered his entire body, including a visored helmet that covered his face. And though his armour was made of gold and copper, and was studded with diamonds, what he offered was a platter of bones.

To Mahmut Abdullah, this vision signified failure, that it was his destiny never to be rich or well-known. Success had eluded him and life was only meant for struggle and fighting God. What baffled him was that despite his closeness to God, he felt betrayed by Him. He prayed every day, but with rancour in his heart.

Then one night, something different happened. The soldier knocked at his door again in his dream, and once again he opened it. But this time, the plate was not filled with bones. This surprised Mahmud Abdullah, who asked the soldier where the bones were. The soldier revealed his face and spoke for the first time. 'In Darwa,' he said. 'The bones are in Darwa'.'

The guide continued the story, 'It is said that the soldier was none other than Mahmut Abdullah's future self, and

Darwa was the very place we stand today. Darwa was where Mahmut Abdullah found the bones of 1st-century humans, with which he began his dream to bring into existence this great museum. The guide directed us towards a glass box in which were two bones, placed on a copper plate. 'One is of a man, the other of a woman,' said the guide.

I looked at Hyder. He looked as mystified as me. I had not realized before the significance of dreams. Dreams have life. They have answers. They are symbolic. They represent the metaphors of life. We are never disconnected from anything in the Universe. Something is always awake inside us, even when we are asleep. The story of the museum also made me wonder if there were dream-weavers appointed to appear in our dreams as messengers.

And by then I could also see that Hyder knew the answer to what I had asked him that morning: 'Where are we going?'

The answer was *dreams!*

✢

CHAPTER 34

365 Days of a Sufi

Month Nine

I was curious about the bird and its flight. Following the insight and the sign, I walked up the hill. It was a simple and peaceful place. I was rather breathless from walking all the way up to the community space, so I quickly found a bench to sit down, overlooking the city.

As soon as I sat there, a lovely woman came to me with a jar of water, a little boy by her side. 'Water,' she said, handing me an earthen cup and poured into it cold water from the little jar. It was my saviour. I looked at her and smiled. She was a pretty woman, wearing a light brown headscarf which covered her shoulders. Her eyebrows met above her nose and her honey eyes shone with a deep sense of contentment. Her long eyelashes almost brushed the skin of her cheeks. She looked to be a well-composed and peaceful soul.

As I drank from the cup, the water felt cool going down my throat – a blessing in that searing heat. 'Thank you,' I said and smiled.

The little boy by her side offered me a piece of *baklava* from a packet in his little hands. Then they bowed to me and moved on to offer water and *baklava* to the other travellers who had climbed the mountain.

There were many people sitting, walking, chatting, or listening to the whisperings of the wind and enjoying the beautiful view of the city below. I too, sat there feeling calm, looking around at the cedar and pine trees, and the little stream burbling its way downhill. In the distance, I saw the flags of various towns fluttering atop poles. Then there were hawkers, selling fresh and dry fruit. Afar, a few adventurous souls ambled to the end of the mountain trail.

In the centre was a large open space, roofed with palm, pine and coconut leaves. Inside, people sat in silence, some writing, some meditating. It was a place for those who wished to find some freedom and peace, to feel the love of nature, and like me, to reflect and ponder upon life and its purpose.

At the time, I was also pondering on death. For the past few days I had been feeling very close to the thought of dying, that the next moment could be my last breath; that the next minute I could be in a completely different world. I led the ordinary life of a common man, knowing that I had been raised by a humble man who had a treasure that fuelled me with knowledge, courage and *ibadat* for the rest of my life. Sitting on that mountain, I recollected those precious moments in Pena, the lake where my mind and heart had decided to go on a journey someday, alone. And here I was, living a bit of that dream.

I still wondered if there was something called *fate*. Where would I go once my life ended here? What was the celestial world like? What was it like in heaven? What was it like in hell? What was it like to emerge into another world? What was it like to experience the ultimate *fanaa*? A series of questions reeled out in my mind. I was grateful I had had the chance to journey with Musa, to walk peacefully along the same roads that he and my father had taken as seekers.

As I sat there, the woman who had given me water came up to me once more, with the boy, and informed me, 'It is about to start.' She hurried away to tell the others.

What was about to start? I wondered. People began to gather in the central space. It was certainly a large concourse of people, though some chose to remain aloof. I got up and joined the gathering. It was pleasant sitting under the leafy roof. As everyone settled, a charming young man, perhaps in his early twenties, rose to welcome everyone.

'Thank you for joining us. Today, angels from Heaven come to Earth to meet us humans.' His voice was spirited and enthusiastic. There was a humble elegance to his posture. Poised, he spoke eloquently, 'There are countless experiences and stories that prove angels have visited humans in many forms, be it in the form of good news, a vision, in prayer, as a bird, a guest, or just a message in a dream.'

I was instantly reminded of the mystical bird that had sat on my window that morning; a sign towards the next step of my life. Apart from going to the nearby markets and local stores, crossing the little mounds that were peculiar in the town, and an evening stroll alongside the poplars, I rarely ventured far from home. But these mountains had called to me; I had to be there. The bird had indeed been an angel.

'We are here seeking *Haqiqa*; the ultimate truth.'

The young man's locution caught my attention. I was gripped with curiosity about what was to come.

'And while one walks miles looking for it, yearning for it, praying for it, all the time one is holding a piece of it within. What you look for is already a part of you.'

The boy, who seemed no less than a *dervish* to me, began to recite *Sufi* songs, his tenor voice tinged sweetness and devotion for *Allah*. As we got tuned into his melody, he slowly began to whirl, a fascinating offering in gratitude for the beautiful gathering and the day. As he spun, his robe would rise up and then swiftly fall, and before touching the ground, it would pick up its breath again. He spun around, his right hand raised to Heaven, and his left pointed to the Earth.

It was the first time I had ever seen a *Sufi* whirling. It was the first time the glory of trance opened for me and from it came, the air of light, the streak of love and the stroke of the soft sacredness of divinity. My questions about dying seemed to slowly disappear into the world between the worlds. There, in that moment, there was no dying, no living, just merging into the source of the undefined ecstasy. The mellifluous voice echoed, reciting the name of *Allah*. I would say it was one of the best moments of my life. *Allah* felt more close to me or I had surrendered myself into the presence, beyond words.

Tears ran down my cheeks in the fullness, kissing the whispers of love that my heart was feeling. There was grace and eloquence, effulgence in his smile, and a deep devotion and piousness in his whirling. The more he whirled, the more empty I felt – a *fakira*. In those moments I had a glimpse of Musa and felt the presence of my father, Hyder. I leapt into the realm where the past and the present meet, face to face. My heart ached at the sight of my mother. I was blessed, I thought. Life itself seemed the reason why I was here, and death just another existence.

Watching the young dervish's impeccable love and search for the ultimate truth, I was mesmerised and inspired to experience *more* love. As he whirled I felt my being freed. His devout presence filled the space. I was overwhelmed yet peaceful at the same time; pain and pleasure befriending each other. There, I felt no escape; neither from life nor from dying. I had not known that someone else's meditation and devotion, their seeking and love, could open the path of truth in my heart. And then, as his honest movements took on a slower pace again, I caught the sound of my own breath and slipped into the stillness within me.

As the *dervish's* pace slowed, everyone's eyes were moist, in awe of what they had just seen. A few seconds later, I heard the crowd applauding in the same rhythm as he spun. The youth rested his hands on his heart, bowed graciously in all four directions, and thanked everyone for their presence. Many of us stood up in respect for his selfless gesture that had given us the chance to experience a deeper love of *Allah*. He sat down in the same place he had whirled, as if it were the centre of the universe, gathering his breath, his eyes closed. There was a thoughtful smile on his face as if *Allah* was still smiling upon him. He breathed easily, despite the fact that he had just performed an intense dance.

'I perform each year on this day,' he said, opening his eyes gently. 'And the reason behind this is to add *more* love to this world.'

Indeed, I felt more love.

He continued, 'When I was little, I used to hit a boy at my school. That boy was innocent and naïve. I often bullied him. But, instead of responding with anger, he simply offered me his tears. One day, during the lunch break, I punched him really hard on his face. He just stood there, numb, his face turning red, tears pouring down his face. I was so close to him that I could see his tears oozing out, not from hate, but hurt. His eyes silently asked me only one question: 'Do you realize that what you are doing is a sin?' I felt shaken by those silent, tearful eyes, and I could feel his pain in my nerves. I was ashamed of myself. I was petrified by my own grandiose ego. I contracted within and my heart yearned for his forgiveness.

That day, I went home and fell sick for many days. I have no idea how the little soul of mine could feel so much pain, so much guilt, that even apologising to the boy seemed futile in comparison to my bitter actions towards him. I cried in my mother's lap that night, barely able to confess what I had done.

A few days later, my teacher came home to see me. I was in my room, alone. She looked at me and held my hands, and as she did that, I felt all my sins being forgiven. I could see in her eyes that she knew what was exactly transpiring within me. I may have been young but my soul had the ability to see and feel things deeply. The guilt of being a sinner and the pain of having hurt someone opened a new door of love in my heart.

That day, my teacher told me a little fable, holding my hands the whole time. And since then I never miss the chance of telling that story to whoever I can. The fable was called, *A Magical Dream.*

Once upon a time, two celestial angels sang harmoniously, waiting for the Goddess to arrive. As happened every year, on this very day they met the Goddess, who would bring them a new message.

'I wonder what message the Goddess brings for us this time,' one of them said, barely able to contain her excitement.

Suddenly, a magenta light spread across the sky. The angels could hardly believe the final moment had arrived. Their Goddess was here. They bowed and sang Her praises,

'We welcome you, O Divinity! You are the most merciful, gracious and virtuous. All year we have waited for this day and now that you are here, we are filled with great joy and awe. Your beauty and grace are beyond compare. We are humbled by your unmatched wisdom and generous heart. We are ever ready to obey and serve you. Please tell us the new message you bring. What do you wish us to do this year?'

The Goddess looked at them lovingly. 'My bright little angels, you have always obeyed my wishes. Every time I ask you to do something, you make it happen. This time, I have a unique and special task for you. Your journey will be long but novel.'

'We are ready!' the angels chorused eagerly.

'So listen carefully, my angels. I want you to go to Earth this time, and bring me the most beautiful thing from there. Go to every nook and corner; fly over the mountains, penetrate the thickest forests, swim the oceans, and walk long miles on the sands. Find me the most beautiful thing on Earth.'

The angels were delighted. 'We shall certainly bring you the most beautiful gift from the planet Earth. It will be the rarest of rare. Our journey shall be novel, and our eyes shall scan all Earth. We shall bring you the most exquisite of gifts and do whatever we must to fetch it to you.'

The two angels embarked on their journey in search of the earthly gift. Earth was full of precious things. The oceans were vast and gorgeous, the mountains tall and grand. There were enchanting forests, filled with life and serenity. And the beauty ripened and transformed with the turning of the seasons. The angels held their breath as the flowers bloomed and wilted and the grand old trees changed colours. They watched the beasts and birds migrating across the length and breadth of Earth. They moved nimbly from one place to another. The angels could not resist watching the golden sun rise each day, casting a halo over the whole world, nor the shy appearance of the moon and constellations in the night sky. They were awestruck by Earth.

And then they saw the human-made world — the mansions and machines, the great towns and cities. There were little and big villages and thriving settlements, hidden away from the rest of the world. There were great bridges and imperial structures. They watched the airplanes and new inventions every day. They understood that humans were keen to learn everything, be it about celestial bodies or tiny creatures or outer space. The world was overflowing with wisdom and knowledge. Earth had curiosity and courage.

Everything fascinated the angels, but they could not find a befitting gift for their Goddess. The days passed and their search continued...

One day, the two angels sat overlooking a valley. They listened to the roaring sound of a waterfall, admiring its fierce beauty. Shafts of sunlight fell on a village in the valley. Soon they saw a group of people, speaking in hushed voices; some were crying. The two angels rushed to the place immediately. They saw a man was being punished by the King. By now the angels had also seen suffering and strife on earth. They had seen grief and penury. They had seen natural disasters and destruction, disease, famine and death too. But when their eyes fell upon this scene, of one human being's cruelty towards another, it filled their hearts with misery. They could feel the man's agony.

Mushtaq, the red-bearded King, was cunning and brutal. People called him 'the stone-hearted one'. He was unfeeling and oppressed people for petty causes, punishing the innocent. King Mushtaq bullied the people and took great pleasure in their suffering. For many years his cruelty continued in the valley and the people were terrified of him. He was a heavily-built man with a deep, booming voice. His fierce, bloodshot eyes instilled fear in the strongest. His presence filled their hearts with hopelessness. Children ran and hid at the sight of him.

All this worried the two angels. Their gentle hearts could not comprehend such savagery.

'We must do something about King Mushtaq,' said one angel.

'Let us watch him. Let us try to discover what his intentions are, why he harasses the people. We might get some clue from that,' replied the other angel.

The sun had almost sunk below the horizon and the stars, lurking behind the clouds, soon made their way into the dark sky. The two angels reached King Mushtaq's palace. Outside, was a large garden. And in the mellow light of the lamps that had been lit at eventide, the angels could see flowering plants and fruit-filled trees. The plants were precisely pruned and the bushes finely trimmed. The angels had seen many gardens across the world, but they had never seen such a carefully crafted garden as this. It reminded them of heaven. It was an astounding view.

Soon, they heard King Mushtaq snoring, much like a lion roaring. As they went closer, they saw with great astonishment that King Mushtaq was dreaming a beautiful dream: He was watering the plants in his garden. He was singing and talking to the trees. He caressed them and nourished the soil with loving hands. He planted new seeds. No one could ever have imagined that the stone-hearted King could possibly do anything good, or even knew how to love nature.

Suddenly, the two angels thought about their mission on Earth. What could be better than gifting this dream to the Goddess? Who would have thought that a man who harassed his people could dream such a beautiful dream? That was indeed a beautiful thing!'

So the two angels decided to take his dream to the Goddess. They ascended into the all-encompassing sky. And on reaching the Goddess' court, bowed reverently.

The first angel said: 'Oh Divinity, we have finally found a gift for you. The most wonderful thing on all of Earth. Novel, magical, beautiful. Beyond our imagination. A dream of improbable love. A garden filled with flowers and fragrance.'

The second angel presented Mushtaq's dream to which the Goddess said, 'Grant this man a palace of heaven. A single seed of goodness can reap heaven for the world. It is love that brings good actions to the world.'

The Goddess of course, knew it all. 'Dear angels,' she said, 'go back to the man and tell him he can do no harm to this world. He is granted a palace of heaven and he is bestowed with a second chance. Tomorrow shall be a new dawn for him and for the people of the valley.'

Once again, the angels descended to Earth. They went to King Mushtaq's palace and saw he was still asleep. Gently, they entered his dream and appeared to him. In their melodious voices, they sang: 'Oh Mushtaq, you are most fortunate. The Goddess has accepted the offerings of your garden and grants you a palace of heaven. This palace of heaven is nothing but the world around you. Just as you nurture your garden, nurture your people. Mushtaq, the Goddess places her faith in you and offers you a second chance. The new dawn is a call for you to love everyone.'

The angels danced to the music of love and then departed.

When morning broke, King Mushtaq's eyes were filled with tears. He felt the pain he had caused the people of heaven. He understood the angels' message. He could not believe that he too, could be pure of heart, generous and loving. Tears of joy flowed down his face as the Goddess' forgiveness touched his soul.

Soon, he invited the people of the valley to the garden he had tended with so much love. They arrived, their hearts full of apprehension, unable to believe what they witnessed. They saw the King smiling and rejoicing. Though they were overwhelmed by the sight of the garden, they wondered if they were being tricked somehow.

King Mushtaq broke the uncomfortable silence that fell. 'My people,' he said, 'you see how beautiful this garden is. So is this world. We are all flowers of this beautiful garden. Today, I thank the Goddess for bestowing Her gracious blessing upon me, so I could realize my purpose, and my true being. My people, I apologise to you for my cruelty in the past, my unforgiving nature and my egotistic acts. Pray forgive me. Help me start a new journey.'

The angels witnessed this transformation. They were so happy. The King's apology was sincere; his humility genuine. He bared his soul in seeking his people's forgiveness. There was sincerity in his voice, truth in his eyes. And his people believed him. 'He had been touched by the grace of the Goddess,' they said, their hearts full of reverence.

In the palace there were celebrations to mark a new beginning. Thereafter, King Mushtaq built schools, hospitals and homes in the valley. The kingdom became exemplary in the world. Today, the valley still shines with heavenly peace.

'Such is the magic of love and forgiveness,' whispered one angel to the other. They sang songs of love and glory and took off to their celestial abode, rejoicing at the completion of their mission and wondering what the next year would bring!'

CHAPTER 35

The story narrated by the young *dervish* on the mountain that day touched my heart deeply. It was evident that a great sense of purpose had come into his life early. A purpose I couldn't ferret out in myself even now. There was ebullient freedom in his spirit and sweet sweat of love in his heart. It was seen in the way he performed with such éclat.

I learned that for any human, three things are essential – *purpose, freedom,* and *love*. However, it is love that strikes first, then we are nudged with questions about the purpose of life, our individual dreams, and then we are prompted by awareness and the need to experience freedom. I believe that no matter what we do in life and in which order it happens, these three will always remain the orbit defining human life on Earth. And if we experience at least one thing closely, the other two will follow. The three are looped to each other.

Well, having realized this, I knew I was living the last and precious years of my life. I had the freedom now, I knew about my purpose – to *write* – but I wondered if I loved enough. The young *dervish* had left me open to my own sense of vulnerability, questioning aspects of my life yet again.

My wife and I loved each other very much. Together, we had a beautiful son, who grew up to understand his own sense of freedom, and chose to lead his life away from his family. I have a beautiful grand-daughter, Zaitoon, and she is like a million stars in the sky to me. She will shine in this world; I know it. She will know what I am talking about in my journal – about being human and about freedom. Of love, and of dreams. I write this book to let her know that it is possible to live life fully. To let her know, how our ancestors lived.

Now that I am finally coming into close contact with death itself, and I feel responsible to write, to keep alive the stories of our forefathers; their triumphs and struggles; their yearnings to seek for *more,* their relentless efforts to stay close to *Allah.* Perhaps, this is what stories do to us. Musa's words about his journey with my father are woven into the sinews of my being, forming the strong knots of my existence.

Stories fill our spirits. They cause us to question and reflect, mull over our existence and bring lessons into practice. And when we translate the lessons into actions, we become part of what is called the *law of reciprocity.* Stories urge us to reciprocate life in ever better ways. Unknowingly, we bring stories into each other's lives even as we are in the process of making another one in that very moment. Our lives are flecked with the tales of people, and those stories are flecked with experience.

Later that evening, I got into a conversation with the same beautiful, honey-eyed woman who had fetched me water on the mountain. Her name was Gulrose. I sat beside her on a bench in the community space, gazing at the city below and the far-off mountains. The sun had mellowed and its soft rays touched the row of poplars in the city. I shared with her, the story of my life. I told her about the quirky bird I had seen that morning and the message it had brought me.

'It is not your aloneness that will lead you to freedom and enlightenment,' she told me after hearing me out patiently. 'It is what you do in your aloneness. Everybody knows the alchemy of love. But few know that it is not actually the alchemy of love that makes things beautiful and meaningful, but the alchemy of *more* love.'

'But when alone, I am able to recall all the encounters of my life and to forgive myself and other people. It is in my aloneness that I am able to remember God quietly. I do my *zikr* each day, in the morning and in the evening, and whenever else I feel like it.' I explained.

Gulrose asked gently, 'Who are we to forgive?'

'Are we not responsible for forgiving those who have hurt us? And should we not make it happen before we leave the world forever?' I asked, looking at her, a little puzzled. I wondered if I had missed a piece in the puzzle of my life.

Perhaps she read my thoughts for a gentle smile appeared on her face. 'I too, was like you – confused in my ideas about life. But that changed some years ago.'

Gulrose then shared the story of her life: 'I come from Azra, a place from where war never leaves. Every day people flee to the borders, escaping from the callous gunfire and bombing. Soldiers are ever-present; scouting everywhere all the time. My husband died there, in that strife. And just like that I became a widow and a single mother.'

I was stunned to hear of the hard-bitten events of her life, despite which there was no trace of anger or resentment in her voice or in her eyes. She seemed to have healed from the terror and grief she had faced, through no fault of her own.

'A few years later, my son fell very ill,' Gulrose continued. 'I had no money for his surgery and the doctors declared that without it there was no hope for him. It was an emergency. Once again, my life came to a standstill. Life began to ebb, exposing the old scars I had learned to seal in order to take care of my son. While he lay in a makeshift medical facility, the gentleman in the next bed talked to me, trying to give me some solace. He asked me my name and where I lived. When I reluctantly told him, he took a closer look at me and asked if I was Nasir's wife. Of course, I was taken aback. This was the first time I had found someone who actually knew my husband by name and family. I replied that I was indeed Nasir's wife.

He then said something I will never forget: 'I am a soldier. I am the person who shot your husband.' I could not believe my ears. The man was crestfallen, full of guilt and shame. I could see in his eyes that his confession was sincere and his apology ingenuous.

I took a few seconds to gather myself. And though life seemed fraught and fragile, and the old scars opening afresh, the pain I had doggedly suppressed inside me gradually receded. I said to him calmly, 'Listen carefully to what I am about to tell you, soldier. You might think it strange but I want to thank you for what you did.'

As expected, he was astonished, even alarmed. Perhaps he thought I was insane. I maintained my composure and told him the truth about my life. 'Yes, the man you shot was my husband. But every day we were together, he killed me, bit by bit. He was a sadist who abused me and my son every night. He never loved us. My heart was wretched and my life sombre and unpromising. I feared for my son's life and his future. So I thank you for freeing us.'

I looked into the eyes of the man who had killed my husband to ascertain my truth. It was uncanny to meet him like this, but my soul greeted his soul, which seemed humane to me. All of a sudden, this confrontation released me from the weight of the sour thoughts and the scars I was holding in me.'

When Gulrose finished narrating her story, she looked at me with her beautiful eyes and said, 'And so I ask: Who are we to forgive?'

My judgements seemed to break their barriers in the presence of a woman who was not only courageous, but also acknowledged the existence of pain and struggle. I asked curiously, 'What happened then?'

'Today, that man is a good friend. He gave life to my son. Not because he shot my husband, but because, even in that moment, he did his duty. He helped me with the surgery of my son, and I can never be grateful enough to him for that. He had killed what had been taking away my life, and gave life to someone who only creates love and life in me.

And so, my friend, living alone is not meant for sitting and remembering this and that to forgive. Living alone is about befriending those for whom you can create *more love, more freedom, more dreams.* It is about making friends with those who need friends. That is the reason I choose to be here. I come often, with my son, to spend time with new people; to serve them water, and feel the freedom of being human. We only get old. Not alone.'

Those were her last words to me before she left with her son, leaving behind for me a beautiful memory. Her story urged me to look differently at my own life.

Never again did I see that bird that had brought me to the mountain. But I recall it often – to remind myself that I am still here, and still capable of being a friend to someone.

PART V

CHAPTER 36

Meru sat cross-legged, a yarn of cotton-polyester cloth spread over the mat on the terrace. A wooden hoop held a corner of the fabric tightly. Meru's hands were busy with the needle and threads, weaving in and out, forming little by little the design of a bird with extremely long feathers.

'Is that a peacock?' Zaitoon asked. She was sitting beside Meru, watching every move of the needle and admiring the precision with which Meru was creating the design. Zaitoon made sure there were no pleats in the cloth as the wind swept through at intervals.

Around them, were many kinds of beading needles, double-holed ones, tapestry needles, a couple of wooden hoops, various threads, hooks, scissors, and the paper Meru was referring to for the design. Several other design workbooks lay open as well.

'Yes, it is,' Meru answered.

'Why a peacock? Is it in fashion now?' Zaitoon wanted to know.

'I have sewn many like this one, but all different in pattern and colours. Many people think the peacock symbolises vision. It is a symbol of good luck, you know.'

'Really?' Zaitoon gazed at the tracing paper.

'Who drew this?'

'Most people know the design they want and bring it along with them as a reference. And with them they also bring their stories. I cannot remember any customer who did not have a story behind what they wanted. To add to that, some people are very specific and persuasive. Sometimes it feels almost as if getting a particular design is a matter of life and death for them.'

The friends chuckled at this.

'I can imagine that some of them must be very set on what they want,' Zaitoon said, still observing Meru's needle moving in and out of the cloth, leaving a tiny piece of the design on it.

'It says a lot about their personalities too,' Meru added, cutting the thread and loosening the cloth from the hoop and shifting it before fitting the frame again. 'First, you must have the whole design in your head. Then, part by part, you bring it alive through your threads, always keeping the whole image intact in your mind. And then one fine day, the whole of it is finally on the cloth. A replica! There remains no piece in your head to be transferred. It feels complete. And your mind is empty.

When it looks even better than in your imagination, it is very satisfying. And when you see the same shine in your customer's eyes, you know you have done your job well. For Gulfam *Kaka*, it creates more profits, and more referrals. However, it is more fulfilling when a customer has only a vague idea and relies on your creativity. Then it is your original creation. In those cases I often sense the person, even in my sleep. Walking down the grey streets to the shop, colourful designs start forming in my head.

Now that I think of it, those old narrow streets have given me so many different ideas. Something tells me what the customers would like, and what they will not. Often, I do not even meet them directly. It is a relative or friend who comes to place the order. But even in such cases their likes and dislikes are so clear to me that while my fingers are busy weaving from my imagination, it feels as if I know them personally.' Meru paused, took a deep breath, wiggled her fingers and then raked through her hair, tucking a long strand behind her ear. She straightened her back, craned her neck left and right, and then resumed her needlework.

Zaitoon could see how Meru was able to multitask; talk with her and produce the design at the same time. It seemed like second nature for her friend. It was a quiet practice, Zaitoon thought. Indeed, weaving was meticulous work and Zaitoon was inspired by Meru's creativity. One had to be focused and dedicated to the work. Zaitoon admired Meru's tenacity.

After a few moments when all that could be heard was the rustling of the leaves on the trees, Meru said, 'One day, an engaged couple came to the shop. Such a thing rarely happens. Usually, the parents of the bride and groom come with the bride-to-be, to get the *zari* work done. But this young couple seemed uninhibited and open. They wanted both the shining and plain threads to be used together. Gulfam *Kaka* was surprised, as most young women preferred the shining threads and flamboyant designs.

The young couple explained that they met during a very rough time in their lives. But if it had not been for the struggles and uncertainties they were confronted with, they would never have met, nor found love. Though those days were behind them now, they were grateful to have found each other.

Thus the plain threads would represent the difficult times and the shining ones the great times born from those hardships. They wanted the shining threads to remain intertwined with the rough ones, so that they would never forget the nature of life. They could never forget that it was in the moments of greatest strife that love had been born, and now they were to marry each other.

I was much too naïve about such things then, but I understood that what they were saying was not trite, but honest and genuine. Though they did not share the details of what had occurred, the gist was enough for me. I saw their connection and unwavering bond. And watching them I had some inkling of the fact that what I produced would be an important symbol of their union, and that I would somehow always remain a part of their lives, in memory.

Their story and their faces often came to mind while I designed for them. I would talk to them in my head whenever I was in doubt, and listen for answers.'

'Were they happy with your work?' Zaitoon asked, her eyes wide with bubbling curiosity.

'When they saw the spangled design over the borders and the rough threads neatly woven with the shining ones, they were more than delighted. They felt the design depicted the history of their shared lives. I was pleased.'

$\mathcal{S}$

CHAPTER 37

Musa's Tales

Almost three and a half months had passed since Hyder and I first began our journey. Hyder was as content as God could be, but I was not there yet. I had not got closer to God but I was certainly closer to Hyder and for me, his presence kept me close to myself. It was interesting to observe this aspect of life. If one doubts one's own closeness to God, one can be with someone who seems to be closest to Him. Being a witness to Hyder's unfolding journey, I felt I was the luckiest man on earth. I found myself easily succumbing to the idea of love, to the idea of peaceful freedom, and to the thought that I had yet to find my beautiful purpose.

We slept on the roadside, under bridges, in temporary encampments, and in the homes of kind people who offered us a night's stay. We sometimes took siestas under the cedar trees and rested our back on logs. We dipped our feet in clear streams and rivers and inhaled the fragrance of flowers blooming in woods and gardens. We ate raw fruits and at times went to sleep on an empty stomach.

I wasn't used to such measures in life, but I was free. On our walking journey, there were times I felt miserable and sometimes, I was very much at peace. The questions *Who am I?* and *Why am I here?* often crowded my mind. They seemed to perch in my thoughts permanently. I struggled with the fact that I was clueless about my life's purpose. It bothered me. I thought that those who knew their dreams and challenges were more blessed than those who had yet to find them. Such thoughts continued to gnaw at me. With each passing night, sleeping under the open sky or under the quivering trees in the cold, I wondered, *What was I doing with this man Hyder? What else could I do with my life?*

One evening, we joined a group of gypsies travelling from Aerkona to Maklaw, a distance that took three months to cover on foot. The gypsies hailed from the forests of Aerkona, and were migrating because their master had a premonition about a wild storm that was to come. It was time for them to step out of their sheltered abode and expose their skins to the heat of the soaring sun.

I asked the Master of the gypsies why they set out on such a long journey under the sun to settle in tropical Maklaw?

'We are a tribe of Nature,' he replied as we sat around a campfire, later that evening.

The temperature had dropped markedly, considering how we had sweltered during the day. We all huddled around the campfire to keep warm. I was extremely tired, as was Hyder. It was nearly midnight but Hyder did not want to miss this chance of exchanging thoughts and ideas, and extending the boundaries of his knowledge. He only had time until sunrise to do that, as by then the gypsies would have already sowed their souls in another land. In the many months of travelling with Hyder, I still did not know what God was, but I did understand a little what a lover of God could be. And perhaps that could, in itself, be a path to enlightenment. I was beginning to understand one more thing – that I was capable of something *more*. What that *more* was, had still to appear on the radar of my destiny.

'There are basically three things in life that we, as a gypsy tribe, remember and remind each other of, at all times,' the Master said.

'What are they?' I was curious now.

'They are not unknown or mystical, but they are magical. One – each human being's ability to walk on the path that is their purpose; to keep walking; to keep travelling despite having their roots somewhere else in the universe. A tree can grow only when it moves away from its roots, though it is never disconnected. We are not meant to be stationary.

Second – keeping the love alive within. We are a tribe of Nature; all Nature on this entire planet; we are Nature. We cannot, in any way, be disconnected from love. Yes, we may get disillusioned. That is the nature of love itself. But it is also love that clears the way. Only love brings humanity together. We remind each other of love and that it has to begin with us.

The last thing, what we all seek, even though it is etched within us – freedom. We all seek freedom at least once in our lifetime. Freedom is the ultimate principle. Giving freedom to someone is the greatest blessing from God. Only humans have the ability to seek freedom, to engage in freedom and to impart that freedom. No matter what we do or where we go, these three things remain our trinity for life. Whether we seek them deliberately or not, these three tenets are engraved within us.'

'Your precious gems of wisdom make their way into my mind like bitter medicine. I feel both encouraged and miserable!' I exclaimed. 'You say we already have these three things within us, yet they are the very things I am looking for. I do not feel them inside me. Are they not inscribed in me? And if they are, where are they?'

I could feel a sense of failure growing within me. I felt deflated. 'Who am I?' I cried, unable to stop my misery from flowing out. 'Who are we?'

The Master looked at me, his eyes calm, filled with the wisdom of experience and insight. 'Young man, these questions that come rushing forth from deep within you have only one answer. And that answer is in *Noorah*, whose life has been handed down to us by our forefathers, the Masters of Nature. We sing about his life to every growing child in our tribe.'

The night was getting cold but the fire of new knowledge kept us warm as the Master narrated the age-old tale.

'A long time ago, in the land of fairies, there lived a vivacious flying horse called Noorah. The horse was as white as snow and had dove-like wings that were swift and magnificent. He could fly a thousand miles in a matter of seconds. With his intuitive powers of love, speed and sharp vision, he took great care of his land, which stood around the base of a huge mountain. Sitting on the highest point, on his throne, he looked resplendent, radiating light and compassion for the people of the land.

One day, Noorah was sitting atop the mountain as usual, observing his land below. Suddenly, dark clouds hovered over his head, looking sinister. They hung heavily around Noorah, making him feel dizzy and unstable. He realized that the heavy dark clouds were invaders, wanting to blur his vision. They had evil intentions. Noorah had no idea where they came from and why they were interfering with his work.

'O Dark clouds! Perhaps you have lost your way,' he cried. 'It is I, Noorah, the guardian of this beautiful land. Please let me be, for I must watch over my people.'

But those monstrous clouds would not heed him. In no time, they had tethered him from every side and begun to pull and push him. 'We will not let you be!' they roared. 'The land will not be at peace! We will rule the land, not you.'

'Making people suffer is not a wise way to rule,' Noorah said, unfurling his powerful wings to fight off the clouds. 'The only way to live in people's hearts is with love and peace.'

The clouds howled again, 'We will trap their hearts with darkness and rule them through fear. We will be powerful. They will be our slaves. We will rule the world. We will rule Nature. You shall not stop us sitting here on the mountain.'

Noorah fought with all his might, but the clouds were too many and too dark. They attacked Noorah with vengeance. For days and nights the fight went on. But there came a moment, when Noorah was weak and disoriented, his energy lost. That was all the clouds needed. Quickly, they seized Noorah's heart. The monstrous black clouds defeated the flying horse and he fell from his beautiful royal throne down to the land he so loved and had protected for eons.

The next day, under the stifling sun, Noorah found himself in a tattered heap, lying at the foot of the mountain. *Where was he?* His vision was blurry, his skin muddy, his mind delirious. He reeked of dried blood. He shook his head and ran his fingers through his wild mane. He had turned from a vivacious horse into a human! His bare feet hurt as he walked, trying to recognize the place and the people. He stood there for a while and just stared at everything and everyone. It was a vast landscape with thatched huts and houses, bazaars, shops and hawkers. Children played while men and women walked the streets, all lost in their own world.

Noorah's eyes spotted a man sprinkling water on the tomatoes in his cart. 'Sir, what is this place?' he asked, clearing his hoarse throat, the words barely stumbling out of his dry mouth.

The hawker stopped, gave him a confused look and went back to sprinkling water on the tomatoes.

'What is this place called?' Noorah asked again.

But the man did not turn. What language was Noorah speaking? Neither the hawker nor the other people around could decipher it. Life became tough without communication. Days passed as Noorah observed the people, busy with their chores. He decided he could not keep wandering about aimlessly, timelessly. Hunger pinched at his belly.

Noorah became a sweeper. It was a job that didn't require him to speak much. He swept the market streets and shop floors, people's homes and gardens. He even went door to door to collect trash and dispose of it in the dumps.

He cleaned the decrepit houses and isolated places which others refrained from visiting. Noorah did not hesitate to do anything that would keep him engaged. He survived with minimal wages but became well-known for his sincere work. Months went by in this way. Noorah was no more than a layman doing odd jobs to survive in this land of people.

One day, Noorah was engrossed in sweeping the market streets when a few tomatoes came rolling his way and stopped at his feet. When he looked up, he saw a young woman walking away. The bag she carried was torn in one corner and the vegetables she had bought were spilling out from this hole onto the road as she walked.

'Excuse me!' Noorah called. 'Your bag…it is torn! The vegetables are falling out, madam….' As soon as he uttered the words, he realized their futility for the young woman could not understand him.

However, she did turn around. And stood still. She stared at Noorah for a few seconds, then asked, 'What did you say?'

'I said…' Noorah was about to repeat what he had said but before he could do so, she screamed in delight, 'You speak the language of the mountains!'

The young woman spoke the same tongue as Noorah. He couldn't believe his ears. 'So…you understand what I'm saying?' he asked, bewildered.

The woman smiled and nodded. She stood there, as bemused as Noorah, her eyes gleaming with joy and her heart filling with unimpeachable conviction. Serena. That was her name! Blue eyes and a perpetual smile on her face.

Her sable-black hair flowed onto her shoulders. Her features sharp, yet precisely genteel. Her energy was vibrant, bubbly. And the colour in her cheeks deepened as she spoke to him in her dulcet voice.

'I finally found you, Noorah! I finally found you.' She seemed relieved and excited at the same time.

'What?' Noorah asked, puzzled.

She dropped her bag and began to dance around him. Her blue eyes stared at him from head to toe. She giggled like a child who had found a secret treasure.

'O Noorah, my Master, you are here!' Serena exclaimed, still dancing in delight.

'Who are you and how do you know my name?' he asked, surprised.

Serena lived on the land to protect the people while Noorah sat atop the mountain. Protecting the people by living like them was her mission. She led a very simple life, teaching calligraphy. Finding Noorah, her Master, was the greatest reward she could have desired. She was aware of his magical powers and that he was a magnificent caretaker who healed and protected the people. Their mission was the same.

But Noorah retained no memory of this, so he thought that Serena might be crazy, even dangerous. He quickly turned away and resumed his sweeping, hoping she would go away if he ignored her.

'Do you remember who you are and where you have come from?' she asked him in a clear voice.

Noorah continued to ignore her, certain now that she was a dangerous woman who would drive him crazy too. He thought she was plotting something against him. Full of foreboding, Noorah asked the blue-eyed girl to leave him alone.

Yet Serena followed him saying, with her hands stretched out, 'Noorah! I have an answer for you. I can help you remember who you are.'

Now she had Noorah's attention. He stopped sweeping and looked into her eyes.

'Do you remember how you came here?' Serena probed.

But Noorah had no answer. His heart was laden with confusion. 'Do *you* really know?' He stood there irresolute, a part of him hopeful.

'Yes,' said Serena, 'come with me.' She grabbed his arm and walked along the narrow street.

'Where are you taking me?' Noorah was hesitant but he kept pace with her.

'You will know once we get there,' she said.

They continued to walk through the town, past the markets, gardens, huts and houses, and open green fields, till they finally entered a silent bridle path bordered with trees. Birds chirped sweetly.

Noorah had no idea where they were going or what she was going to do to him. Doubts and fearful thoughts niggled at his mind. 'Where are we going, Serena?' Noorah asked rather sternly.

'We are nearly there,' she assured him. 'Do you like it here, the peace of this place? Come, let us listen to the cooing and trills of the birds. Let us hear the song of the wind. Let us stare at the sky while it weaves its magic around us.'

Soon they reached a quiet lake, facing a panorama of huge mountains, beyond which the sun was about to set. Noorah marvelled at the beauty of the place while Serena sat down on a rock watching the hilltop with fondness.

'Sit down there,' she said to Noorah, directing him to another rock.

'Why are we here?' he asked.

'Have you seen yourself?' she asked, ignoring his question.

'What does that mean?' Noorah grew impatient. 'Will you just tell me who I am and stop asking these strange questions?'

'But Noorah, to know yourself you must see yourself,' Serena insisted. 'Come,' she stood up and held out her hand to him. At the water's edge, Serena said, 'Look into the water'.

Noorah did so, knowing there wouldn't be any straight answer from Serena. He could see his own reflection, but it was unclear. 'Now what?' he asked.

'Look into the reflection of your eyes in the lake, Noorah. Look within,' she urged him.

The water reflected his eyes clearly. He looked into them.

And as soon as he did so, the wisdom of the world began to unfold before him. He saw a ray of light beginning to glimmer in his eyes. His body shuddered and his eyes shone. He was drawn into spirals of light. There he saw revelations – about his self, his roots, his mission, his magical powers, and Serena, with whom he could fulfil the purpose of his life. Memories began to surface, bringing his trapped powers back to him.

Noorah's body began to tremble as his heart re-ignited. The darkness in him retreated as the truth emerged. He felt lighter and lighter. Illuminated, he remembered his wings, snowy and luminous.

As he looked up at Serena, he saw the same glint in her beautiful blue eyes. There was a blaze of triumph in them. It was a celebration of their togetherness. Realization about his true self dawned and along with it, his beautiful wings. Noorah looked up to the top of the mountain and there, his enigmatic throne waited for him to take flight.

'I thank you Serena, my beloved!' he said, feeling the power in his wings.

'We will continue our journey together, to protect this land,' said Serena, her eyes welling as she embraced the moment.

Noorah opened his wings wide and flew up over the turquoise water into the crimson sky. He flew into the sunset, away to the great mountains, to reclaim his place on the throne.

Serena waved till he was just a little dot in the sky. *There you go…to sit on the throne of wisdom and light again,* she thought.

Noorah soared higher and higher and finally arrived on his throne. Once again, he was Noorah, the magical horse, who protected the land with his benevolent magic, love and compassion. As he sat looking at his land below, a beautiful realization enchanted him – that all humans on the lands were angels, just like he was when he fell from his throne. They were fallen angels too.

'Fallen angels!' he exclaimed.

He had a new mission now. It was to help the people look within and find the light in their angelic hearts. Noorah looked up at the moon, while Serena enjoyed the silhouette of the mountain, and prayed for her beloved.

Once again the land was at peace, under a million stars.

CHAPTER 38

365 Days of a Sufi

I came back from the mountain completely inspired, as if someone had infused a new zest for life into me. It was like a rebirth. After meeting Gulrose, I felt a new animus in my soul, something I had never imagined I possessed. The first thing I did was to discard the thought of dying that had hovered over me each day. I had assumed that my life, alone in this house, was dedicated to God. I was wrong. I was so wrong.

My life was dedicated now to humans. I was committed to using my gifts. So *write* is what I had heard and *writing* became my purpose and *written* became my committed love for humans. It was a simple interchange – dedicating my life to people and committing to the gift *Allah* had bestowed upon me. I already had the tool to stay close to *Allah* – *writing*.

When I returned to my lone room, I was a different man. Not lonely at all. The whole world seemed to be my abode. I began to wonder whether my actions could give people a little solace from their miseries, and help them experience a little freedom? And thus it became my understanding: the alchemy of *more* love leads to freedom, maybe to the ultimate truth. As the *dervish* on the mountain had said – *haqiqa*.

One more thing – I write this more as a reminder to myself than anything, that the ultimate freedom is not experienced at the end of our lives; it is experienced while living, while we are still alive. It is simple. Give someone a tool to live their lives; share your gifts with them, and see ultimate freedom come alive.

Each day, love grows and that brings your Beloved closer. Thus the alchemy is in *more*. I cannot say I am a seeker yet. I am a novice. An amateur. I am just a practitioner of being a seeker.

Ibne-Al-Rashid, February 1900

Ramadan! The holy month had begun. As every year, Sakina *Khala* was eager to clean the house and help the two girls prepare for the celebration. It would be their first *Ramadan* in this new house. How elated all three felt by the atmosphere of festivity in the city. Although it was still two days to *Ramadan*, the city was ablaze with new gest and gaieties.

The girls washed the curtains, cleaned the rooms and dusted the walls. Even the huge frame with the Prince was brought down to the floor to be carefully cleaned off with wet and dry cloths in turn, making sure the frame did not break. Meru looked at the gleaming eyes of the young man in the painting, his gaze fixed as if watching a loved one at a distance. Was the loved one in his imagination? What had his life been like?

Meru's thoughts filled her mind while Sakina *Khala* was warming the fresh milk to make *firni*. The aroma reminded Zaitoon irresistibly of the happy times of her childhood. 'In our village, *Ammi* prepared *firni* for all the neighbours,' she said. 'She was known for it. Indeed, it has always been her speciality. She prepared it in a big pot and the sweet smell would waft through the house. Children would gather hungrily outside, eager to try it. Relatives would flock in with succulent dishes, sweetmeats and dry fruits. It was such a lively and jubilant time.

I remember Khalid *Kaka*, my favourite uncle, visiting us every year, bringing the most generous gifts. He was my *Abu*'s childhood friend. I never saw my *Abu* spend as much time with anyone as he did with him. When he came, he stayed with us for four or five days, and the two friends would just sit in the verandah and talk for hours together. Sometimes they would go boating on the small lake which was located on the outskirts of the village, getting away from worldly matters, out of the sight of the hullaballoo of the festivities and distractions.

When they sat on the verandah, sipping tea and homemade savouries, *Ammi* would sometimes join them. She called him Khalid *Bhaijaan* and he would bring lovely gifts for his Sakina *Aapa*. The two shared a great camaraderie and Khalid *Kaka* was very protective of my *Ammi*.

I would be overwhelmed with the toys and clothes he brought for me. Khalid *Kaka* worked in a big city, for a wealthy aristocrat family. He was their caretaker-chauffeur-cook-gardener, everything. He was a trusted and honest man. The whole village would gather when he drove in, in his van. He would drive us around in the evening. I still remember those moments when the crisp wind would blow on my face, and the tantalising smell of freshly baked bread, sweetmeats, *biryani*, *kabobs* and steaks would float in the air. As we drove along, the children would run behind us until the van reached the main road and picked up speed.

I would enjoy watching the wide skyline from the thicket of alder trees on either side of the road. Every villager would respectfully call a *salaam* as we drove along through tiny villages and small towns. Sitting in the car, I would dream of the big city he came from. He often told stories of its plazas, people, promenades and bazaars. I would imagine myself walking in its gardens and around the ponds. Since then, I was determined to live in the city someday.

Khalid *Kaka* was such a hero for me. I can never forget the cheerful ambience he brought with him during *Ramadan*. He had the most innocent and cheerful smile. His chubby cheeks still held those little innocent dimples when he smiled. I would count the months, weeks, days and hours for him to come. He told me that the family he worked for had a daughter my age. She always reminded him of me.

'I don't have my own family. *You* are my family,' he would tell my *Abu*.

Once, he also suggested that we move to the city with him; he would find work for *Abu*, and it would be good for my education. The wealthy family he worked for would help me get into a good school. But *Abu* merely shook his head and chose to stay put in the village, preferring the calm, natural way of life. He believed the education in the village was fair too. He disliked the hustle and bustle, and the fastidious pace of living in the city. Moreover, he did not wish to be indebted to Khalid *Kaka*.

Though I was little and did not understand much, I would often hear arguments between *Abu* and *Ammi* on this subject. *Ammi* was keen to move, to lead a promising life in the city, but *Abu* always diverted the conversation. In my heart I was angry with *Abu* too. I wanted to be in the city and go to school there.

Over time, an estrangement crept into *Abu* and Khalid *Kaka*'s relationship. Abu considered him to be a bad influence on me, making me think of what was not in our means. He could see I was attracted by the superfluous stories of the city. *Kaka* felt uninvited. It was insinuated that we all felt the same way, including me. Khalid *Kaka*'s visits became infrequent, and then stopped. Thereafter, there came only the basket of gifts from him, and one *Ramadan*, I remember I waited the whole night for Khalid *Kaka* and the gifts to arrive, but they did not come.

Despite the sorrow of breaking the bond with *Kaka*, *Ammi* often remembers her brother and continues to celebrate *Ramadan* with the same zeal. And she prepares *firni* and *sheer khurma* for everyone.

Ramadan is a chance to connect with people, Meru; to make new friends and acquaintances. Celebration is enough reason to get to know others. Whatever the struggles in life may be, on this day we forget all about it and enjoy ourselves. At least that is how it used to be in our village,' Zaitoon reminisced fondly.

○

Listening to Zaitoon, Meru was reminded of how quietly even *Ramadan* was celebrated in Bashirbagh, though the children from the grimy alleys often lived like life itself was a *Ramadan*, no matter the situation they found themselves in. Most of those urchins wandered about, dallying on the streets the whole day while their parents struggled to earn enough to feed them. Those children were left to the mercy of God and Time, Meru thought.

'Which world are you lost in, Meru?' Zaitoon asked, laughing.

'I was thinking of going to Bashirbagh for *Ramadan*. I feel like celebrating with the children there. I can make sweetmeats, and some friends.'

'No, Meru,' Zaitoon immediately asserted, 'you are celebrating it here with us. It is our first *Ramadan* in the city, in Otto. Besides, it will make *Ammi* happy. Look how she is on top of the world for the past two days. See, how well she is progressing each day, walking and moving more.'

Meru looked at *Ammi* in the kitchen, watching over the boiling milk. 'Listen how she is humming. I'm sure she is remembering Abu and Khalid *Kaka*.' She could not justify her intention of going back to Bashirbagh. The friends continued to clean the house until the evening. The two bedrooms upstairs were largely untended as Meru slept on the terrace, while Zaitoon slept on the floor next to *Ammi's charpoy*. The rooms needed a thorough clean.

'Meru, I want to give you something for *Ramadan*,' Zaitoon said, cleaning the wardrobe in one of the bedrooms. Through the window, the world outside looked cheerful. The street hawkers called out about new sweetmeats, toys and clothes. At the curb, a small merry-go-round had been set up for the children to enjoy the holiday. There was also a candy-man who enticed young and old alike with his inviting pink and yellow candies.

'Please tell me you will not turn away the gift,' Zaitoon pressed.

Meru was silent, yet exhilarated.

'I would like you to pick one of the bedrooms for your own and stay with us forever,' said Zaitoon in a rush, clasping her hands.

Hearing this, tears came to Meru's eyes. She felt overwhelmed. A knot formed in her stomach and her heart skipped a beat. There were mixed feelings. She was afraid she was getting used to the city and would never be able to return to her little house, to the small town of Bashirbagh, where she had grown up; the place that held all her childhood memories with her parents. This made Meru anxious. 'I am but a fallen angel,' she murmured.

'So am I,' Zaitoon quipped.

Meru looked outside the window, contemplating the generous gift Zaitoon was asking her to accept. There, on the other side of the street, the Children's Home still stood, undecorated, uncelebrated and silent. Her thoughts drifted to the paradox of life in Bashirbagh, where children, despite living on the streets, roofless, celebrated freedom, while this Home, despite its place in the city of Otto, seemed hollow and friendless, disengaged from life – a paradox Meru was experiencing within herself too.

'Don't you remember Meru, that fallen angels have wings too?' said Zaitoon quietly. 'They have merely forgotten how to spread them.'

The night was quiet. The city had gone silent. Meru lay awake in her new bed in her new room, alone. Yes, it was her room – a fact that was hard for her to accept. Would she be staying here forever? Was Zaitoon's family her family now? Had Zaitoon become her sister rather than a friend? Meru's thoughts continued to linger on these points as moonlight shafted through the window and fell on the wall opposite her bed.

There, in a small frame, hung a painting of birds, flying from a pier towards the sky. Several small boats were tethered there, while several others seemed to have left the quay. But they were all empty ones. The image was small but so intricate in its detail that Meru found something new and interesting every time she looked at it. It didn't look like a normal dock where the boats were stationed. It seemed to be a private place. A promenade extended along the waterfront from the small palace. Some birds sat on the flag-pole that fluttered over the little boats. Although it was just a painting, the presence of the strong gusty wind felt real. *The painting has lost its life*, Meru thought. *The colours have faded over time and the frame has lost its patina. It looks like a relic as if the original was painted by some artist in the 17th or 18th century. Maybe earlier.*

Her mind returned to the series of events that had taken place recently. She lay still on her bed, conflated between thoughts and emotions. She lit a candle and placed it on the window sill. She opened her notebook, turned to an empty page, and began to write her first letter.

My loved Ammi and Abba,

How are you? I miss you. See, I write now. A little bit. I miss our home. I live in Otto. Zaitoon and Sakina Khala love me very much. This house is very very big. I feel I am in a dream. Ammi, tell me it is not a dream.

Gulfam Kaka is getting old. He is worried about my marriage. He tells me to get married. I am not ready yet. I want to go to Bashirbagh, but Zaitoon says no. I do not know what to do. What is right, Ammi and Abu?

Sakina Khala is making firni for Ramadan. We will share it with the neighbours. We will make new friends. I think it is a very good idea. I miss you, Ammi and Abba. Can you come back? Please.

Allah Hafiz Ammi Abba.

Meru

And as the moon gazed down from its starry screen, Meru felt proud of her writing, her heart raring to living more merrily.

$$\mathcal{S}$$

CHAPTER 41

Meru felt exhilarated. It was the first time in many years that she had seen her *Ammi* and *Abu* in her dreams. She sat with Zaitoon on her bed, both sipping hot cups of tea. The morning sunlight filtered through the slats of the window. Outside, a florescent orange sky blended with silky streaks of magenta and pink.

'I haven't felt so rested in many years,' said Meru. 'It was like I had been teleported to a world where the people living on earth can meet those in heaven. You know, I actually felt they were with me in the flesh.'

'Tell me more,' Zaitoon asked curiously.

'I saw throngs of people gathered for some festivity. I could not tell which place it was but it seemed similar to the Otto bazaars, or the one described in the book in the city of Pena. There were so many people assembled, waiting for loved ones at the fountain. I saw a Sultan. I don't remember his face but he said we had only eleven minutes and eleven seconds to meet our loved ones. And from a beautiful gate of heaven, emerged my *Ammi* and *Abu*. I was surprised, crying in my sleep. My heart felt full. It was beating faster. I felt the palpitations. I couldn't believe my eyes! They both looked like their younger versions, their skin shone with health and their shoulders were firm. Their nails were pink and their lips held youthful smiles. Perhaps the water in the heaven is so pure that no one ages there. You know Zaitoon, I feel grief eats up time and makes you older than your age.' Meru reckoned, lost in her thoughts.

'What happened then, my friend?' Zaitoon recalled her friend from her reverie, wanting to hear more.

Meru's gaze returned to Zaitoon's face. 'I don't know how, but we were at some quay, the boats were stationed. Perhaps it was because of this little painting that hangs here. As if I was a part of that painting in reality, not in my dreams. *Ammi* and *Abu* had brought some grains they had earned in heaven and they fed the birds, the geese and the turtles. They gave me some to sprinkle around, telling me to use the grains wisely. Before the seeds had even touched the ground, a flock of mysterious birds which I have never seen in real life, flew in and pecked on them.

Ammi said it was a good sign. In her eyes I saw trust and assurance; what about I could not tell. She was not angry with me, or upset. I always felt they left me because I was not good enough; that I had done something wrong. But now I know that is not true. I saw *Ammi* was well; that she and *Abu* were both at peace. Then they sat in one of the boats and went away. But even as they departed, I did not feel scared or lonely. I waved happily. I knew I would meet them again. Then I woke to the innocent sounds of the day – the chirping of the birds, the whooshing of the wind against the window, and the scuttling sound of cycles in the street.'

'That was beautiful! See Meru, I told you they are happy, and that you are not alone here. They can see that. Now, you live with us,' Zaitoon said with irrepressible gladness.

'Zaitoon, I woke with so much peace in my heart. Although the Sultan said we had just eleven minutes eleven seconds, I felt I had talked with them the whole night. To my surprise, it was enough. I feel content,' Meru said. Deep inside she knew the dream was an answer to her first written words to her parents. She felt reassured that she now had a new way to connect with them.

CHAPTER 42

Musa's Tales

By the sixth month of our journey on foot, Hyder and I had eased into it. We were more relaxed, more centred in our faith. At this point, there were a few things about which we felt sure – that no matter what, we would find a way to continue our journey; that we did not have to worry where our next meal would come from; and that miracles would certainly cross our path.

I had stopped missing my home by now. Instead, I focused on what was to come. Of course, I had yet to figure out my purpose. But I knew I was a seeker. Another thing I knew in my heart was that Hyder was not only a *Sufi*, but a *Sufi Master*. But he was far too humble to admit it. He kept saying, 'I still have a long way to go'. But I had witnessed his journey all these months. The realizations that took me a long time to achieve, Hyder would already have them before we even began to veer in that direction. He walked the path as a realized being. I, on the other hand, was always in limbo. Sometimes, we argued about our different ways of approaching the world. Not that I was always wrong. He appreciated my decision to leave behind all material comforts and find solace in life's rugged beauty and the vastness in which we were but tiny dots.

During our travels, we were once beside a silent lake. We

spent the night there, sleeping on the grassy bank. I now found it easier to sleep out in the open, under the stars. The boundaries inside me were disappearing. So were the terrains and borders I had acquired while growing up. I was beginning to get a closer view of life. Silence had finally seeped into my soul. I understood that our quest does not really begin with the question: *Who am I?* Getting to this question is a journey in itself.

The following morning, we sat beside the lake, dipping our toes in the cool water. We felt soaked in the serenity of its soothing flow. The sky reflected its giant presence in the pellucid waters, with smoky clouds marching across it. The grass was covered with a shiny mantle of dewdrops. Not too far, hills lined the horizon. It seemed like we had reached the end of a journey and there was no place in the world left to go. And on that shore, while my mind was consumed with watching the universe around me come alive and feeling that perhaps, finally, I would meet with some miracle, magic, or God himself, Hyder began to narrate a tale he had heard from his *Sufi Master*.

For years, an eagle went to a saint and asked him the same question: 'Where and when can I meet God?' And each morning, the saint would look into the eyes of the eagle and smile. He would then turn his gaze to the rising sun, engrossed in the sights, sounds and fragrance of nature. The saint said nothing to the curious eagle.

Then, one day, frustrated by the saint's silence, the eagle decided to take it upon itself to find God. *I have waited long enough for the saint's answer*, the eagle thought. *I neither understand his silence, nor do I get why he sits every morning on the cliff, looking at the birds and trees and mountain*s.

So the eagle flew off on an expedition to find God.

Its first halt was a small cave on top of the mountain. The bird was delighted. *I'll definitely find God here,* it thought. Looking around, the eagle saw a monk sitting and chanting with his eyes closed. The eagle approached him saying, 'I am on a journey to find God. I have travelled for many days to meet Him. Since you are a monk, you would know where and when can I find Him.'

The monk looked at the eagle and smiled. His smile reminded her of the saint. 'You can meet God here and now,' said the monk.

The eagle looked around but saw no one, only mountains and rocky cliffs. Nothing else was in sight. 'Where is God?' the eagle asked, perplexed.

'Here,' answered the monk calmly.

The eagle was annoyed at this response, thinking the monk was too selfish to share the details and wanted to keep the secret for himself. The eagle flew away with a heavy heart, but still determined. The eagle continued her expedition, flying for days together, barely sleeping. Each day, when the sun sank, the eagle's heart sank too, in loathsome despair. *Why is God doing this to me? Does no one know where He is? Am I a sinner that He cannot even hear my voice?* it wondered.

One morning, flying over a village, the eagle heard the bells of a church ringing and a choir singing. The eagle landed atop the church and waited for mass to end. When everyone went away, the eagle approached the priest. He was sitting silently with his hands crossed, looking at the flames of the candles placed at the altar.

The priest greeted the eagle cheerfully. 'Hello, my dear. How can I help you?'

'I have come a long way to meet God,' replied the eagle. 'I hope to find Him here. I want to meet Him, right now.'

The priest looked at the impatient bird and smiled. 'Your answer is in your question, eagle. God is here. And He is here now.'

The eagle looked around. Again, there was no one. The church was so empty and quiet that the eagle could hear its own breath. *The monk said the same thing. He said God is here and I can meet Him now. How is that possible? If He is here, then how can He be in that cave too?*

'I don't believe you,' said the eagle to the priest.

'God is here and now. You can call Him,' the priest repeated.

'But how?' asked the eagle.

'Close your eyes and sit peacefully in silence.'

'You are lying. You are fooling me. If I close my eyes how will I see Him?' The eagle was beginning to lose its temper. It did not know what to do and felt hopeless. Looking around in vain, the eagle could neither see God nor hear Him. And so, once again, the eagle flew away on her journey.

A few days later the eagle heard the *muezzin* reciting the beautiful *azaan*. The eagle flew in that direction and sat on the onion dome of the mosque. 'Good evening, Sir,' said the eagle. 'I have come from very far. I am on a journey to find God. I heard you reciting prayers. You must surely have met God. I too, want to meet Him. Can you tell me when and where I can find Him?'

'You are right, my friend, I meet Him every day,' said the *Imam*.

'Where?' asked the eagle eagerly.

'Right here,' answered the *Imam*.

'What? You mean God is here? Then I can meet Him now?'

'Yes, absolutely!'

'But if God is here and I can meet Him now, then who was it in the cave and in the church? How is it possible for God to be at different places at the same time?'

Once again the eagle was confused and frustrated. This time it did not look around for God. The eagle felt empty and helpless. Its search had been futile. The eagle was annoyed. *No one knows where God is. No one can show me the way to God. Maybe God doesn't exist at all. Maybe everyone wants to keep this as their secret.*

The eagle decided to give up the search, though this upset it even more. Gathering all its sadness to itself, the eagle flew skyward, higher and higher, beyond the clouds. It went faster and soared higher than ever before. Suddenly, the eagle began to feel light. Its anguish turned to freedom, and its flight became effortless. Subliminal peace surfaced in its heart. The eagle became aware of everything – its wings, its breath, its eyes, its overflowing heart, and the pure air.

Never had the eagle enjoyed its flight so much. Its soul sang gaily, its mind relaxed. Its wings were dancing and the eagle felt blissful. Looking down, it was mesmerised by the beauty of what it saw. The entire earth looked one, and small – the cave, the church, the mosque were all one. There was no difference in their appearance. They all looked like flecks of grain. The eagle understood why each holy man had said the same thing. From high above, everything was the same – both the journey and the destination.

Tears of gratitude filled the eagle's eyes. It had found profound peace and beauty of its own being. It found God within. The eagle realized it was one with everyone and everything. The sun was ready to set once again. The birds were returning to their nests. The crescent moon was showing its beautiful face, and the stars garlanded the sky. The eagle felt the presence of heaven.

The eagle returned to its home on the cliff, content and exuberant. The saint was still sitting where he had been. 'I finally met God!' the elated eagle told him. 'I finally found Him!'

The saint's eyes twinkled. The spark was always there in his eyes but the eagle had missed his divinity till now. From that moment on, the eagle and the saint became sacred friends. They accompanied each other in silence for hours, experiencing life around them.'

When Hyder finished the story, I looked around too. The sun was bright and the water sparkled as if a thousand diamonds lay shining before us.

Hyder said in a clear voice, 'When one sits across the ocean, when the horizon is far yet visible, when one sits on the mountain, when the valleys go deeper than our hearts, I feel the presence of my purpose. Nature reminds me of the gift of life. But even when I am in the hustle and bustle of the cities, in those thin lanes where life is louder than heartbeats, I see the same truth of my purpose in the eyes of everyone I meet. People are my reminders. Reminders of this gift of life.'

Of course, I did not know then that what he meant to say was that even if we go far from the world, Allah exists both there and here. Here with me and there in my city, and right under the roof of my regal palace. *Life is not just about listening to stories, but about creating one's own too, isn't it?* I said to myself, letting the deep silence take over between Hyder and I once again.

PART VI

CHAPTER 43

Meru and Zaitoon sat on the old wooden bench in the small cave-like office of the Children's Home. The colourless walls, the dark rooms, the rusting wrought iron railings outside, appalled them. Some of the floor tiles had broken, the holes temporarily filled with gravel. In the middle of an atrium, a small mosaic fountain stood forlorn, yet a reminder of past beauty. Though the structure was large and had a distinct elegance to it, the place had lost its numen.

The two excited friends sat across from a young man, perhaps in his late twenties. His name, he told them, was Zaroon. They offered him the *firni* as a gesture of goodwill, wishing him for the day. It was *Ramadan* finally, and the girls couldn't be more thrilled to have filled their morning with meeting neighbours, offering sweets and wishing them well, and in return, making friends and acquaintances and receiving blessings from their elders.

Zaitoon looked beautiful in the silk headscarf Meru had embroidered for her. Had it not been for that particular fabric, given to her by her *Ammi*, Zaitoon would not have been reunited with Meru. That headscarf was a motif of their friendship, their reunion.

'Thank you for bringing us this *firni*,' Zaroon said in a soft voice. He had a genteel smile on his olive face with its protruding forehead, narrow nose, elongated almond-shaped eyes with grey ringed irises, like the new moon. He had a slim figure, a long neck, and bony shoulders. His long fingers brushed back the lock of hair that fell into his eyes. His demeanour was humble, well-mannered and sincere.

'My *Ammi* made this. It is her speciality,' Zaitoon said, feeling a sense of pride as she said it.

'Happy *Ramadan*,' Zaroon replied with a pleased smile on his lips.

'We live across the street, right there! You can see it from here.' Zaitoon pointed to the old house, now alive, which stood on the other side of the street. They could see Meru's room from where they sat – a place in which she had finally begun to feel free. A bright yellow curtain hung across the window. Meru realized that as much as Zaitoon's home was beautiful inside, it had a pictorial charm and quaint history from outside too.

'Please have some,' Zaroon said, placing a dish of dates and figs on the table. 'This is all I can offer you at the moment,' he said sheepishly.

'Oh, that is more than fine.' Meru muttered in her low shy voice. 'Would you mind telling us about this place? Only if you don't mind,' Meru added.

The place indeed reminded her of Bashirbagh as the voices of the children resonated, much like those near her home, and the dark prosaic rooms were strangely akin to the dark, lonely alleyways at night.

Zaroon said that he looked after the administration of the Home, but more than that, he was a mentor to the children.

Some called him *Bade Bhaijaan*, and some of the little ones called him *Baba Jan*. He was a delight to them; someone in whom they found solace, someone in whom they could confide their feelings and lies.

'I too, am one of them,' Zaroon told the girls with a small smile curving his lips at the look of surprise on their faces. 'I was very little when I was rescued. I was homeless but I didn't grow up hopeless. We are children of the war, a group of young girls and boys who were brought here by fate. Some lost their parents, some got separated from them, some were victims of war. But they were all homeless. Many of these children have grown up to be responsible adults and have started fresh lives. Some alumni are as old as eighty years of age. They visit us when they get a chance, and they support the Home in little and big ways.'

Both Meru and Zaitoon listened to him attentively.

'We face many challenges here. The City Council has given up on us. Resources are scarce but we manage to feed every child, and of course, they have a roof over their heads. We are one big family. What we lack is freedom and good *talim*. We need that. The world is progressing. You see what I mean?'

The two friends nodded soberly as he continued to speak. Perhaps he wasn't just a friendly soul but also had the gumption to make use of his position in a better way.

'No one sticks around long enough to teach us and bring real change in our lives. Life is stagnant here and sometimes crushed and crumpled too. It has been eighteen years since I came here. As much as I can, I try to look after the younger ones, find resources and people to support us.

We want the children to attend private schools so they gain admission to good universities in due course.'

The girls listened to the young man, himself a survivor of life. Meru understood the pain of feeling abandoned, the loss of parents, and the grief, plight and fear of not having anyone in this world to confide one's deepest sorrows and sadness. But she also knew the magic of fate, of finding a friend, and the possibility of change such as she had experienced. In that moment, Meru knew that this place was the beginning of her new life connection. She found resonance with the home, while Zaitoon could also barely hide her empathetic emotions as Zaroon continued to chronicle the challenging lives there.

'This city of Otto was nothing less than a place for royal families, emperors, kings and queens a hundred or so years ago. You see these structures are so old and yet so regal and elegant. Kings and Princes would have at least one residence here. They say that this place where we are sitting now was the first big library in the world, for Otto was also a city of knowledge. Scholars, scientists, philosophers, artists, mathematicians, cosmologists, and many historians and researchers shipped their work here from distant places. This city had a plethora of old scriptures and manuscripts. Perhaps such enlightenment and education was a threat to those who wished to keep power in their own hands. Thus came to this beautiful city war, conquest and loot.

The public library was set on fire and all the vast knowledge of great minds was lost. But though they burned the books, they could not quench the fire in the hearts of the right ones. A noble family bought this land and built this place. It was their home first, and now to many of us.'

'Where did the noble family go? What happened to them?' Meru could not withhold her curiosity. Myriad thoughts raced in her head. Zaitoon smiled to see how Meru had turned from a taciturn, introverted being into a vocal and confident young woman.

'Well it is said the Begum bore two sons, and according to the norms, the eldest was to become the successor, the heir of the family legacy. The untimely death of the nobleman led to bitter infighting amongst the brothers, all of whom sought the family wealth and position. It led to them killing each other. Bowed by grief and tragedy, the Begum decided to give away all the wealth to the City Council, and stipulated the house should be turned into a Home for children. That is all I know of. Imagine, this place has a history of loss – first the library, then the Begum's tragic life.' Zaroon shook his head sadly, letting out a soft sigh.

'After years of enduring such grief, a generous-hearted King married Begum and took her far away, to the other side of the globe, to a life of ease and comfort. This gave Begum the opportunity to begin life anew. They had a son. He was Begum's only offspring after her earlier brutal experience. The King bought this Home again and lands in this city for his son. He built many architectural marvels. This building was restored. But then, the King's only son took a different path and chose to become a *dervish*. Thus, once again fate stepped in to upend human plans. And this building went into the hands of the City Council once again. Isn't this a long, unbelievable history?' he said. His lips smiled but his eyes were reflective.

'When the library first burned down, a handful of books and manuscripts were restored and placed in the public museum of Otto, until a decade ago. But then the museum sold those books to another museum in a foreign land, and thus, whatever minimal funds we received, also stopped. We can live with the loss of our past eternally inside us, but this place has helped many like me fill the echoing voids of our lives. Of course things have changed, but I believe the legacy of the Begum's kindness will continue. My fate brought me here, but now I too, have the chance to change the fate of many children here. This place certainly teaches one to be patient, humble and kind.'

Zaroon's words revealed to Meru and Zaitoon, a new perspective. The protracted talk moved them deeply. Having heard the story, they were no longer the same young women who had entered the place so blithely with their gift of *firni*. They understood they were not the only ones who suffered loss and pain; that there were those in the world, outside their radar of thoughts, who were looking for love and freedom.

Evening had seeped into the room. This *Ramadan* was indeed different. It was true what Zaitoon had said, that festivities were the only times when people forgot their sorrows and let go of their long-held boundaries and masks. Everyone was equal. It was easy to talk about anything under the sky. People were no longer strangers but each other's confidantés. Everyone felt free.

The city certainly felt more like home to both Zaitoon and Meru that day. They had made friends but didn't know that their friendship with Zaroon would be the beginning of a new direction and widen their horizons. From a small world, they would be part of a bigger world. That they were going to have promising days ahead. The seed of purpose was already planted.

'*Allah* is great.' Zaroon placed a palm on his heart and bowed. '*Ramadan Mubarak*. Please thank your *Ammi* from everyone here.'

'*Inshallah*, we will meet again,' Zaitoon said, bowing gracefully in return.

$$\text{\textcyr{}}$$

CHAPTER 44

Zaroon's world had filled Meru's and Zaitoon's hearts with as much warmth as sadness, and left them deep in contemplation. The unkempt structure overlooking their terrace was no longer strange to them, instead, it seemed numinous. And Zaroon himself had been forthcoming, honest and pleasant. There was veracity in his words and his conduct.

'It is quite clear that Zaroon has a pure heart, don't you think? His words inspired me,' Meru said. 'He could easily leave the Home and walk away to lead his own life, like other alumni have done. But he feels responsible and committed. I guess he makes a good mentor; a good example for the children.'

Zaitoon agreed. 'You know Meru, I used to wonder what I would do in this big house with my ailing *Ammi*, before I met you. I still wonder sometimes how I'm going to lead the rest of my life. But with you I find solace. I feel that piece by piece things are falling into place. I have begun to feel affection for this city and its people. One cannot adapt to the city unless one makes friends with its people, I believe.'

Zaitoon paused for a long time, looking at the wide horizon in the distance, where the sun had almost buried itself in the belly of the earth, to be born again on the morrow. All around there was silence, and there was stillness.

'Zaitoon, when I came here I knew nothing really. But with you, I am now able to read and write a little. I didn't tell you but I wrote my first letter to *Ammi* and *Abu*. I know I must have made many errors but I felt so proud of myself. In fact, I'm sure *Ammi* and *Abu* would be very proud too. I feel ignited with new strength by educating myself. I realize how important good *talim* is, just as Zaroon said.'

After a reflective pause, Meru continued, 'I also learned that knowledge not only comes from reading and writing but *listening*. My own journey started that way. *Listening* to the story of your grandfather, *imagining* going on that journey with Musa and Hyder, *meeting* all those people in my mind, I felt that I too, can be different...that I am capable of choosing my path. I feel I can.' Meru looked driven in spirit.

'Yes Meru, that is the power of story-telling, right?' said Zaitoon. 'A long time ago, people passed on their knowledge through signs and stories, and it continued for generations until writing was discovered. People heard and listened to folklore and fables to learn and understand their lives, or to see what else was possible. Do you know what the first alphabet in Hebrew is, Meru? *Aleph.*'

Meru was curious.

'It is mentioned in the scriptures that once all the alphabets of the world were arguing with God, giving all sorts of reasons why they should be chosen as the first letter in the Universe. All the alphabets were making a great noise, except for one – *Aleph*. And though *Aleph* sounds like an entire word, in truth it is said to be silently hidden in each word that is spoken on earth. It is with *Aleph* that God created the world.

After hearing the pleas of all the letters, God turned to *Aleph* and asked why it had said nothing to prove its importance. Did it not want to be the first? *Aleph* explained simply that since it was *silent*, it had nothing to say. That was its basic nature – silence. *Aleph* has no sound of its own. Indeed, it is used as a silent alphabet. God fell in love with *Aleph's* gentle nature and humility, and declared it to be the first of all letters. Thus, all creation comes through *Aleph* and we silently imbibe its nature.'

'Wow!' Meru exclaimed, much struck by this. 'I never imagined that my childhood friend would come back into my life and teach me what I never even knew existed! Thank you, my friend, for your stories.'

The night settled in as the conversation between the friends continued. In the sky, the stars had begun to put up a great show. Meru gazed up at them and then her eyes drifted to the Children's Home across the street. In her imagination, she could see the children, and Zaroon finishing his duties. In that passing moment, a new thought enlightened her mind.

'Storytelling!' Meru suddenly chuckled. She looked at Zaitoon, wide-eyed and excited. 'How about telling stories to those children?'

Zaitoon looked at Meru, her heart leaping with excitement. In her eyes was the same sparkle as when their paths had crossed, months ago. Meru had found a way to help the children.

'That is a great idea, Meru. And how about teaching them some *zari* work too? Zaitoon giggled.

Meru jumped up. Her feet would not stay on the ground, lifted as if by some magic. To her, it all seemed like a dream she was living, too good to be true. She had never expected her life to turn around in this way. It was pleasant and surreal.

'Let's start by reading them *365 Days of a Sufi*,' Zaitoon suggested.

'That book is truly a gift,' Meru agreed, smiling.

'Zaroon said the place was the first public library. You think history could repeat itself? This could be the beginning of the same again? We could create a library too, Meru.' Zaitoon's thoughts whirled like a *dervish* in full flow. 'And more and more people will listen to and experience the stories of *more* love.'

'*More* is good,' Meru chuckled, her heart beating as if she was racing to the top of the world.

The two friends merrily chattered away about their ideas under the light of the twinkling stars and soft chilly night. New things were on their way.

✍

CHAPTER 45

365 Days of a Sufi

Month Ten

I woke at midnight, feeling thirsty, and rose to get a drink of water. My throat felt parched and my body tired. Walking up that mountain had exhausted me. This was the fifth time I had woken to sip some water. Instead of going back to sleep, I sat down to write. I opened the window. It was a moonlit night. The cool breeze gushed in, as if eager to be home. My home. I looked up at the sky. There were some white clouds.

I remembered the beautiful woman I had met on the mountain, and her story of forgiveness. Today was a day to think differently, I mused. *I must not think of who and what I need to forgive but what and how I must give.* I felt responsible to use my gift of writing. And only if writing could bring awareness, would my living be valid, and my life not just a random whim of God, but an intention of his will. It was true, I had to write.

Looking outside, I saw the clouds pass by swiftly in the moonlit sky. Just as dark clouds show up in our brightest moments, white clouds also linger in the darkest moment of our lives. You are able to see this, provided you are ready to wake up.

I was drawn to the mountain again, to meet Gulrose. She had the same serene composure, serving water to visitors that I remembered. And her little son Junaid looked a day older and wiser. He sprinted towards me with his open arms, and hugged me.

'*Salaam*, Rashid *Kaka*!' he greeted me in his genial voice.

I gave him some fresh loquats that I had bought in from the market in town. Delighted, he immediately began to relish them, sitting on the stump of an old tree on the cliff. I sat on my old bench to rest my tired calf muscles. I watched the gabled roofs of the town below and the blue sky holding wads of cotton clouds. The crisp breeze patted my face. It was a beautiful day.

Gulrose lifted her pail with water and filled the mugs, offering them to the visitors who had come. I must admit that it was impossible for anyone to ignore her beauty, the graceful way she unconditionally served everyone. It reflected her resolute, innocent heart and agile spirit. There was something about her soul that ignited me towards reviving my own life.

'I have a lot of time in hand,' I told her. 'I wonder how I can be of some use to the people here. I know I am old, and not as fit and zestful as you, but I would like to know if I can do something.' I wanted desperately to add meaning to my life and my search. 'My skin may be wrinkled but my heart is far from being deceased.' I laughed.

The woman looked straight into my eyes as if reading my unspoken words and vulnerability. 'A mystic once told me that a time will come when we won't have to make any effort to fall in love with ourselves. We will be born with the blood of self-love. Imagine an era where we are ingrained with *self-love*. Then all our lives can be dedicated to new pursuits, new learnings! We could forget about healing our lives, old scars, regrets and all that, especially when we are ageing.'

She grinned, directing me to let go of my ingrained thought processes of what I must and must not do in my old age.

'You mean I must learn something new?' I asked, trying to make sense of her words in my mind.

'Yes, you need to learn something new, Rashid *sahib*,' she asserted, fixing her eyes on me.

'What could I possibly learn?' I wondered.

'Well, I can teach you something if you want.'

I paused before I uttered in delight, 'Certainly!' Suddenly I realized that learning something is not chastised by time. Any age is a good age to begin something anew. Even if mistakes is all that you procure in the end. Maybe.

'You see I make fragrance, *attar*,' Gulrose said. 'I learned the art from the same mystic who told me about the era of effortlessness. He said to me: *Whatever you do every day, you become that. And whatever you touch becomes that too.* An era of love is only possible if humankind practices becoming *love* through what we do every day. Making *attar* felt cleansing for my being. And when I serve water every day, I feel it invokes a certain sweetness within me, and those I serve.'

Well, that was it. My life changed. I had thought that I would spend the later years of my life alone, being humble in my thoughts. But that was not what was written for me in the diary of *Allah*. I was to meet angels before I left this world. I did not have to end my story. I was to leave my story on this planet in a different way. I was meant to learn something before crossing over to the other world. I was meant to do something *more*.

Attar, I learned to make.

CHAPTER 46

'That was a brilliant idea,' Zaroon said appreciatively to Meru as children romped around the big verandah. They seemed to know only this world, within the walls of the Home, and nothing else.

'This is what my childhood was like too,' Zaroon told them as Meru and Zaitoon looked around the place, bemused.

Many of the children looked up at the girls with innocent smiles and twinkling eyes. Some looked as if they remembered nothing of what happened to them – that they had been left in bins or found lying on lonely streets, or rescued from the violence of war. They had been so little. In them, Meru could see her own life in Bashirbagh. She too had thought the world was limited to her little town and the people around her. The sun, moon and the stars were her own, and no one else's. And now here she was with her best friend, spreading her wings by teaching *zari* work and reading Ibne-Al-Rashid's journal *365 Days of a Sufi*.

'This was my world...small. But as I grew, I felt constricted in this space. I dreamed of leaving this Home as soon I got the chance. The thought pervaded my mind until a wise man with a long *henna*-speckled beard came here to offer food to the children. It was his birthday and I was helping him serve. He told me that it was his 68th birthday, which made it the 24,820[th] day of his life; that he was so grateful for having had the chance to be born. Every year, he visited places like this to share his joy, as he too had risen from poverty and a life of struggle. He came for three consecutive days and in those days he captivated my imagination with his persona and stories.

One story he told was of *Huma*, a mystical sky-born bird. She takes birth in the sky, which is her abode all her life. Not once does she touch the Earth. It is said that her shadow falling on anyone is a blessed omen. I didn't quite understand the meaning of it then and wondered if I would ever have the fortune to lay my eyes on this mystical bird. I certainly wished I would. But now, as I look back, I believe *Huma* had already happened to me through that wise man. Meeting him was the real turning point of my life. A blessed omen!

And there was something he said to me that shaped my decisions from then on. He said that the day we understand our own freedom is the day we realize that the whole universe is our home. I understood then that someday one has to make a choice between staying or going. I knew that when I encountered this question in my own life – I would want to stay. At the same time, I wanted the whole world to come here too – to meet the children, to encourage them to lead better lives. Just as the two of you have shown up.

Help is available, the wise man promised me, observing the rage within me at being abandoned and not wanted by the world. *But the day such questions confront you, you internally know that you have grown up overnight, that you have to make a choice, no matter what...that you are the owner of your own story… your life! And on that day, the choice you make has the power to set you free.'*

Once again, Zaroon's words reflected his openness to bring change into the world of the children who he considered to be his one big family.

CHAPTER 47

365 Days of a Sufi

Month Eleven

One day, after making *attar* with Gulrose, her son Junaid came and sat on my lap. I was rather tired and his warm hug solaced my heart. It nudged the presence of love within me. I remembered my grand-daughter, Zaitoon. As a child she had been the apple of my eye, always so chirpy. It brought delight to my heart to think of her. Her mother Sakina is a composed woman, understanding and docile. She raised Zaitoon well. Ah, I missed those days when Zaitoon would jump up and down, begging to be put on my shoulders so she could pluck the mangoes from those hundred-year-old trees in our village. I remember she asked me to tie a swing on the tree. Every morning and evening, we went along the village road for a walk and every now and then I would swing her up with all my might. She would giggle and chortle with joy. Sakina was anxious lest the child fall and break her head. She did fall a couple of times but that remained our little secret. Grace of God, nothing happened to my Zaitoon!

As Gulrose arranged all the essences, I played with Junaid. I had learned to make *attars* well. The addictive sweet fragrances would not leave my body. The fusion of fragrances became part of my life. Sometimes dewy, sometimes floral, sometimes musky, some balsamic, and at other times fresh and celestial. And if anyone would have asked me what I was proficient at, I would certainly have said: Making *attar*. I especially loved the earth *attars*.

Junaid asked me out of the blue to tell him a story. A story he had never heard before. A story of my own. My weary mind wondered what I could tell him. But I gathered him in my arms, placed him on my lap, closed my eyes and like all the fairy tales, mine began with, 'Once upon a time…'

I took a deep breath and continued, '…there was a little starfish… One day, the starfish decided to go to the sky and meet the stars, the moon and the sun. He had always looked up at the sky from his home in the water and dreamt of meeting them. Every day and night their reflections would glitter in the water. So he began to move towards the sky. He gained this extraordinary power through his strong desire to meet them. He prayed for it every day.

In the sky, he first met a little star. The star was surprised to see the starfish, and that surprise made it twinkle brighter.

'How are you o' twinkling star?' asked the starfish, his voice cheerful and excited. 'I have come from Earth to meet you.'

'But why are you here?' asked the star, puzzled.

'You are so white and so brilliant and you shine so bright! Each night I swim to the surface to see you. You and your friends make a beautiful sight. 'It is my dream to twinkle like you,' said the starfish. 'You are the purest. The most loved one. Everyone on Earth loves you. What is the secret of your luminous light? Where does it come from?'

The star smiled at his innocence. 'If you wish the light in you to shine, then you just have to learn to love everyone. When you do that, your light will also glow. And to love you don't need to go anywhere, you see. Look, I am the Pole Star. I have been here in the same place since the universe was born. People on Earth look to me for direction. If I change my place, they will go in the wrong direction. You understand?'

The starfish nodded, gazing at the beautiful honesty of the Pole Star. 'That is wonderful!' he exclaimed. 'Now I must go and meet the moon.'

Bidding farewell to the starfish, the star said, 'Now, when we come out at night, we will spot you too. And you too, will twinkle down on Earth and inspire others to twinkle like you. And just as we are stars for you, you will be a star for us too. Remember that, little one.'

The starfish waved at the Pole Star and journeyed on to meet the luminous moon. He was thrilled and could hardly wait for the moment he would set eyes on it. The sky was dazzling and shiny. Finally, the starfish came across the graceful moon, who greeted the starfish with affection: 'Hello little star!'

The moon's grandeur overwhelmed the starfish. Humbled though he was by the warm welcome, he also felt puzzled why the moon had referred to him as a star. 'I'm not a star,' he told the moon.

'To me, you are a star. You're a star from Earth, aren't you? Look at you, as vibrant as any star in the sky,' the moon replied.

'Thank you! I met the Pole Star before and it told me to love everyone so that the light within me starts to twinkle. On the way to meet you, I loved everyone in this world. But I did not know whether I was twinkling or not, and the sky has no mirror where I could see this shine in myself. And I doubt if I could really shine as bright as every celestial being here in the sky,' he said, his eyes wide with excitement. 'But I wish I was grand like you. I'm so tiny no one notices me. I want to be like you!'

The moon looked calmly into the eyes of the little starfish and smiled. 'Little one, it does not matter how big you are. What matters is this light. Do you see the light you are already radiating from within you? That is the biggest thing of all.'

'Bigger than you?' the starfish asked, startled.

'Yes, bigger than me too, little one. The light within you and me is the same. In fact, the light within each of us is the same. We may appear big or small to the eyes, but the truth is that it is the same majestic light. I find you big because you live over there, on the beautiful planet Earth. You live with your species and other beautiful creatures around you. You are indeed blessed.'

'Thank you for your kindness, dear moon. Now I will go and meet the sun,' the starfish said, feeling more confident now.

'You really want to do that?' the moon asked, concerned.

'Yes, I really do.'

'But the mighty sun is exceedingly hot. You will burn

yourself. You may even die,' the moon cautioned the curious starfish.

'But I have decided and I will go. I have come this far. I must meet the sun.' The starfish was adamant.

'In that case there is one thing you can do to reach the sun,' the moon said. 'You said that you had loved everyone on your way here. But there is someone you forgot to love.'

'Who is that?

'Yourself!' the moon answered.

'Me?'

'Yes. Once you love and accept yourself for the way you are, nothing can stop you; not even from meeting the blazing sun.'

The starfish felt reassured by the moon's words.

'Go ahead and begin loving, not only others but yourself too. And when I come out in the sky every night, I will see your dreams. They too, will be fulfilled. I will sing songs for your dreams,' promised the moon.

'Goodbye, moon.' The starfish waved, moving up towards the sun.

The more he loved himself, the more he leaped ahead. *This is awesome! I am enjoying loving myself. As I do that, I move effortlessly closer to the sun. This is great!* the starfish thought, gliding effortlessly towards the sun.

Finally, the little yet wondrous starfish managed to enter the kingdom of the holy sun. It looked golden and bright. It was gigantic and its glistening golden rays spread endlessly across the universe. But the starfish neither burned nor died.

'Wow!' the starfish exclaimed, looking around. 'How beautiful!'

'So you finally managed to come. I was waiting for you,' the sun said to the starfish.

'How did you know I was coming?' the starfish asked, perplexed.

The lustrous sun replied, 'Some of my rays were spreading in the direction you were coming from. They saw you coming and told me about your journey. They saw your grit and determination.'

'Is that really true?' The starfish felt elated.

'Yes, it is true. And when I looked towards you, I saw you loving everything in the universe, and I knew I too, was included in your love. And when I saw you loving yourself, I could not resist meeting you. Just as my rays reach out to the world, your love was radiating everywhere, reaching out faster than even my powerful rays. I really had to meet you! It is not just you who travelled to meet me. I too, have travelled to meet you, to thank you for loving me so generously,' the sun said gratefully.

The starfish was stunned to hear this.

The sun smiled at his amazement. 'I may be the sun of the universe, but you are certainly its son too.'

At these words, the starfish felt euphoric! He did not know that just by loving everything, and oneself, things got sorted out peacefully. This magic was in his own hands!

'Thank you, mighty sun,' he said. 'I cannot express the happiness I am feeling in my heart right now. I shall go back to Earth with the star, the moon and you in my heart, to show everyone there.'

'You are the real star, moon and sun,' the sun said, beaming at the starfish lovingly. 'Now little one, allow me to take your leave. It's time for me to rise on the other side of the earth. The birds are waiting to chirp, the trees to unfurl their leaves, and the people to begin a new day. Go, enjoy your sleep tonight. I will eagerly wait for tomorrow, to rise for you again.'

The sun and the starfish bade farewell to each other and went back to their own paths.'

○

By the time the story ended, my legs were numb and my throat parched. But I could certainly feel the presence of the light within. Junaid was still resting on my lap, his head on my heart, his little palms lying softly in mine. He was such a joy to be with. I wasn't sure what effect the story had had on Junaid, but of this much I was sure, the universe wanted to tell me this fairy tale. Not to put me to sleep, but to wake me up. I was still an innocent child of the universe myself. I had forgotten that. I looked at Junaid and thanked him. He had fallen asleep. But I was awakened.

PART VII

CHAPTER 48

'Travellers cannot have habits. The only habit he or she can have is *adapting*. Adapting to everything,' Hyder had told me once.

By then I had learned to write dreams, read dreams, understand the signs of nature, read the stars, follow the ocean waves, grow food, and develop a deeper connection with myself and everyone around me. I was slowly connecting with the alchemy of love and freedom. The only thing I felt I had not found yet was my purpose – the very reason I had left my world in Pena in the first place.

One day, I woke to the thought of returning to my palace. It was the beginning of the eleventh month of our travel, and instead of waking to a new day of journeying with Hyder, I had the premonition that I must return. It was upsetting. My heart thumped anxiously with the unforeseen thought. It took me by surprise and I wondered if our journey was meant to end here, in this way? It pained my heart.

'Hyder, though I feel strongly that I must return to Pena, I am certainly not sure if I really want to return.' My mind was awash in fear.

Hyder was his poised self. 'Are you actually returning?' he asked and paused, looking at me with a grin.

I was silent. Suddenly as I heard those words, my mind seemed to let out a sigh.

'Are you actually going back?' he asked again, this time quietly. 'Or is this a sign for the way ahead?'

I heard him, and understood what he was telling me. But I was unwilling to make my next move. Deep within, I was already feeling the sorrow of separation. My heart felt heavy and tearful. It knew what it had to do and what it had to do did not involve Hyder.

'Will you come with me, my friend?' I asked Hyder, though I knew his answer would likely differ from my desire to be with him. My heart was pining for more journeys with him. How could I go on my own? Everything inside my head started to rumble and whizz, trying to make sense of what was obvious; that which had simply laid itself before me.

'My friend, *seeing a vision of the 'point of return' is a sign* that you are now ready to travel your own path. Our journey was together till here. We must listen to our hearts and the call of our nature, and keep walking where we are asked to go. You remember my journey is also to reach the point where I must decide and choose too. Imagine, my friend, what I am waiting for. What I am yearning for hasn't come to me yet. But it has come to you sooner than you thought. I have to continue my journey in the direction I am called, for as I am on an apprenticeship, and I desire to be initiated by my *Sufi* Master.'

'You mean you will go on your way and I'll be on my own?' My words almost paralyzed me.

'Yes, Musa. That is life, isn't it?' said my friend, who couldn't acknowledge that he was already a master and didn't perhaps need any initiation.

'But…' I began to mutter, but I stopped my tongue. My silence hollered its woeful cries. I knew that no excuse in my head would work; that everything I had learned on my travels with Hyder would now be put to the test. I had to navigate my path back by myself. Soon I would be on my way, and he on his. That moment, I was mooning over my life. I moped. As much I had learned on the path, I also loved my friendship with Hyder. He was my force and inner strength. His presence gave me courage to be vulnerable to the truth. And just when I felt I was almost at the turning point in my life, I felt torn down inside. I have known the feeling of longing. I had longed for this journey. And now, my vulnerable heart lamented again.

We were to bid farewell to each other before sunset. I was haunted by the thought of that moment. However, I wished to make the most of my time with Hyder. That day, we reached a place called Pasha, known for selling wax. There were different kinds of candles, some plain and others with floral fragrances. The market itself was vast. In certain spaces, huge earthen pots were placed to boil the wax in. Many chandlers showed visitors how wax was produced, and sold their mighty candles. Looking at the mountain of wax, I wondered how one lit the wick so high up. At that moment I felt the same about my life. Journeying with Hyder had been like my being in the making, and now the coming separation enflamed me between living and dying.

There, we encountered a wise old man called Baba Bahman, who sat in his small candle shop, observing the crowd milling around with a smile. He was 308 years old – the oldest man in the city. He still sold wax in the market. As Hyder spoke to him, my depressed thoughts rasped in my head, holding me aloof and away from the present moment.

Sensing my despair and melancholy, the old man asked in a warm voice, 'Is everything alright with you, my son?'

'Has it ever happened to you that you were called to return to the same place you left to begin your journey, and that you had come too far to go back?' I asked the wise man, all my vulnerability laid bare. It was obvious from my state that something inside me was melting with sadness.

Baba Bahman began to laugh like a child. 'What do you think I am doing here, my son?' he asked, his eyes shining with wit. 'Where do you think we all come from? And when do you think we will all go there once again, where we came from? What do you think our connection with the Almighty is like?'

His series of questions did nothing to soothe my splintered heart and bruised spirits.

The wise man continued, 'Long ago, I eloped to find freedom. I left behind my family – my wife, my children, and my parents – to lead a nomadic life. I met many great masters who had also left their abode, like me. They had not been saints when they left home. They were just common people. But in the course of the journey, they found people who taught them, told them stories, gave them directions, and helped them walk, until one day these common men realized they had accumulated the wisdom of how to be free. And so it happened to me.

But, once I had accumulated the wisdom of how to be free, it led to another bigger question: What to do with it? And then, on the way, I was struck by the same voice again; the calling. One can call this as tragic or a fate but that which guided me back to where I came from, so I could use the wisdom that I had gained about freedom.

We all forget that we leave a place to seek freedom. Once you have it, what do you think is your purpose in life then? Certainly to return and practise your endeavours with freedom. Practise freedom in your relationships, in your day-to-day connection with *Allah*, in your daily work; and be available to fellow travellers who choose to travel like you, guiding them on their journey.

Do you think it is fair that you chose freedom, gained it, and then you kept it for yourself? My friend, if there is a call to return, know that there awaits your real purpose. That is the magic, the alchemy. That is your home, where many common people may have taken birth to be seekers, like you. I too, faced this point in my life once, just as you do now, my son.'

Hyder and I were engrossed, listening to him. He had many things to share.

Baba Bahman said, 'Then I met a *Sufi* Master who told me a beautiful story. I was as then as young as you, tender of heart and anxious in my belly. The wisdom of freedom came to me only after I had travelled for nearly forty years. Imagine getting a call to return after forty years of journeying?

The *Sufi* Master told me a tale he had heard long ago. It was about a girl who received a doll-shaped candle as a gift. She loved playing with it and grew extremely possessive about it over time. She would give it to no one. She lit it every once in a while in the evening, when no one was around, and each time the girl would gaze in awe of the glowing beauty of the doll-candle, her wonder kept growing. One evening, she heard a friend calling to her. Quickly, she put a large box over the doll so her friend would not see it. The friend came in and they played the whole evening. When her friend went away, the girl lifted the box, only to find her doll had turned black and dark. She was most upset and never found such a doll again.

I understood what the *Sufi* Master was trying to tell me. I grasped that your journey is never yours alone. It is to prepare you for the whole of human existence. And to keep alive what you learned on the way, you need only share it with others. The more you share, the more you love, the more you live your purpose, the more you live freedom, and in that way, the more freedom you have. I also understood that I had never wanted freedom from them; my family, my children or even the world, but from myself. I had never wanted love from them but from myself. And the day I understood this was the day I took the first step of my return. And since I returned, I have sold candles.'

He paused and looked around his little wax shop and said, 'And the one who understands and lives the alchemy of *more* love, remains ageless. Try it, my son. The knowledge in you will only ruin you if left unused. Teach your people the idea of *more* love, and in that you will find what you were seeking in the first place – freedom.'

CHAPTER 49

One evening, after a fruitful reading session from *365 Days of a Sufi*, Zaroon invited Meru and Zaitoon to see the terrace. It overlooked Zaitoon's home. The summer sun was shining bright but it was not harsh. Birds flew in and out of the terrace space and pigeons sat on the heated, semi-decapitated dome. The afternoon was quiet, with few people on the streets and some hawkers at the fork of the road, sitting under their umbrellas, sheltering their fruits and vegetables from the sun. In the distance, the mountains looked like a mirage, their silhouettes floating in and out of some bubble of warm atmosphere.

'When I was a student here,' Zaroon said to his two newly found friends, with whom he had begun to build a camaraderie and connection, 'I always dreamed of coming up onto this terrace. I often asked the caretaker to bring me up, but she would tell me it was a restricted area and that I was too little. The place was dangerous for children. Ha! Indeed! Well, in a way, she was right, for the day I did come here, this place gave me a sense of sheer freedom, and of course, freedom is dangerous, isn't it?' Zaroon looked at the two friends and laughed.

'I know what you mean, Zaroon,' Meru nodded.

'And though this was such a small dream, I had to wait twenty years to come up here. Now that I am here, I look at the world outside and dream my other dreams. While you were reading to the children today, Zaitoon, I thought how beautiful it would be if people all over the world could read such real and inspiring stories. I am learning so much myself! I think it would be a wonderful idea to set up a library of story books here for children.'

'*Yes!* That is certainly a very good idea, Zaroon!' Zaitoon agreed enthusiastically.

'Books connect people. They share both the inside and the outside world, right?' Meru added.

'We can never be alone when stories are all around us,' Zaroon said.

There was a momentary pause as the three friends reflected on their conversation. It had been a long time since Zaroon had felt safe enough to open up about his life to anyone. The two girls reciprocated his trust by listening to his life stories and tales about the children. Every story moved them and each day their interaction became deeper and more introspective. They had come to understand each other unconditionally. And though Meru and Zaitoon were younger than Zaroon, they were able to meet at a common place – their experience of loss and found.

'Your friendship reminds me of my best friend, Ahad,' Zaroon said. 'He and I came to this Home around the same time. We slept in the same bunk bed, we spoke the same language, we played together, ate together, and we had our own little sad-happy secrets. I had begun to find my life again in him and he in me. We made plans for what we would do when we grew up. One was a simple plan to make good beds for all the children here. Another was to sell vegetables. A third plan was to become teachers. Everyday our plans changed. Some days we would joke about escaping from this place, but where could we possibly go?'

A brief yet deep silence ensued as Zaroon reminisced about his childhood.

'I still remember he had these small eyes and red apple cheeks with freckles here and there. A lump of mucus would perpetually lie hidden in the corner of his nose. Children often sniggered and teased him about his large round belly. And then his golden brown hair shone bright in the glaring sunshine. A very gentle and good-hearted friend. He always defended me and would take the scolding for the mistakes I committed. To me, he was everything. Literally everything!

One day, a well-dressed elite couple came looking for him. To my child's eyes, they looked like thieves, come to take my friend away from me. It was an agonising moment. Ahad's *Ammi* and *Abu* had served this family for years. The couple had no children of their own. When Ahad's parents were killed in the war, and the couple found out that Ahad was still alive, they were eager to adopt my only friend. To me, they seemed monsters.

Ahad was torn apart between their love and my friendship. We had zero control of our lives and on our fates. If it wasn't the external war then it was the internal one and separation of any sort is never ephemeral. It lasts for life and you learn to live with it. After he was taken away, I fell sick for days to come. I would not eat, and I turned into an angry rebellious child. The caretakers had a tough time dealing with me.

But this behaviour ended when one day Ahad's letter arrived. It had few words and more of his drawings and scribbles with crayons. I remember the letter was colourful. The drawings showed a big house, a garden, a cat, and a stick figure, which I assumed was him. In another letter, he drew a school and books, and a cat. Another one had just him, standing under a tree, but no cat. For days I kept thinking that perhaps his cat had run away or got lost or even died.

His drawings did improve with every letter. The fourth one I particularly remember, for it had a fountain at the entrance of this Home, and a gravel path. On that path the two of us stood, holding hands. He missed me as much as I did him.

As the days passed, the frequency of the letters reduced. We grew from innocent beings into mature lads. Then the letters stopped. They stopped as if life had moved in a different direction for him, while I remained stuck here, directionless. I sometimes felt angry that he had left me here alone. Surely he could have urged the couple to take me too? In my fury I never replied to him. I never did.'

As Zaroon shared his story, lost in the past, his rheumy eyes shone with unshed tears.-

'Almost a decade later, one day, Ahad came to visit me. I couldn't believe what a handsome young man he had turned into. Those apple cheeks had disappeared, now he had a solid jawline. His golden brown hair still glinted in the sun, but was no longer ruffled. They were neatly combed sideways. He was tall, his belly flat, unlike his former physique about which he had once been mercilessly teased. His fawn-coloured suit made him look like an elite gentleman. I was dumbstruck to find the same love and affection in his eyes as he had years ago for me. I couldn't believe he remembered me, that he had missed me from across the seas, which he certainly could not have crossed alone to visit me before. We embraced each other and talked for hours. He was going away to a Western land to achieve his dream of becoming an architect.

Little did I know that his adopted parents had been supporting this Home for years through monthly donations. Ahad wanted me to join him in his business once he came back, but I never believed he would return once he settled in there. I thought he would get married, have children, and lead a life from which he would never have to look back again. But this was all in my head. He now regularly sends us funds to restore this Home, that had given birth to our friendship. Once we have enough money, we will order new bunk beds – our first plan – which I had since thought silly and stupid. But it is happening. He writes letters to me and now, I respond happily.

Well, seeing you two reunited, reminds me of him. I still have his old letters and when I showed them to him, he laughed at his crooked ugly drawings and messy colours.'

The three of them broke into laughter.

'Where is he now?' Meru asked curiously.

'He lives in Pena. After his studies, he moved there. He says it's a great place for artists and architects.'

'Pena!' Zaitoon exclaimed in surprise.

Meru and Zaitoon chuckled. Pena! Yes, they knew this

place – the place Musa had lived and where he was called to return to. They wondered if his palace still stood regally in the centre of the lake, and if it was still open for people to visit.

'Yes, Pena,' Zaroon confirmed. 'Ahad wrote to me that Otto and Pena had royal ties until a century ago. It was almost like the two places were married to each other. The two cities would marry their sons and daughters, and exchange treasures, art and possessions with each other. He said he would love for me to visit him.'

The swollen sun was becoming less intense now and a cool breeze rose up into the air and blew swiftly across the terrace. The sky was dappled with clouds and the city had begun to come alive after the siesta hour. The rumbling of cars and the loud cries of the street hawkers could be heard all at once.

Zaroon's story had prised open a new door for Meru and Zaitoon. Their days were getting more and more interesting. Although they were listening to Zaroon, their hearts and minds only revved to one thought silently: *Were they to visit Pena? Was this a sign?*

✑

CHAPTER 50

Musa's Tales

That wise old man selling wax also said, 'The only alchemy I found was on my way back. Yes, there comes a point when an ore is completely polished. It becomes a diamond. There comes a point when the metal is totally transformed into gold, there comes a point when a dress is ready to be worn and then there comes a point when you do not need to do anything more. There comes a point beyond which there is nothing more to do. It is a point where the work is simply ready to be used. Thus, you have come to that point now, my son. A point where you use what you created. Use your freedom. Use your love. Use your purpose; open it for the world to use too. The moment your purpose is ready, that is the *point of return*. The moment you bring life to the thing to be used, is the point of *more alchemy*. There can only be *more* of what you create.

Thus, the secret is not about finding it and then keeping it a secret, but in making use of it for humanity. Musa, you have come to a point where you have the chance to use your wisdom. Go back and share it with the world. Tell them about your journey, so others can take a step on their own journeys of *alchemy* through you.'

CHAPTER 51

Ahad's visit changed Zaroon's outlook on life, but it also left him in a state of flux. He was happy for his friend, yet remorse tugged at his heart. He felt that while Ahad was fulfilling his destiny, which was in his own hands, he himself had neither the freedom nor the direction towards his own. Once again, night after night, he could not sleep. Emotions rose up, making him feel useless, and he wondered if a trivial creature like him was just a burden on this earth. Why had he been born at all?

'I went through months of turmoil inside,' Zaroon told Meru and Zaitoon, sharing his vulnerability for the first time. 'Then there came a *dervish*. He lived with us for a few days. He was on a journey to somewhere of which he had no clue. I asked him how he could accept not knowing where he would be the next morning? Was not that kind of life scary? To this, he smiled and said something that remains etched in my heart forever. He said that he was watched over, just as we are all watched over, by *Allah,* who loves us. Our job is to do our daily work diligently. And keep doing it with a pure heart; to keep doing *more*. If you cannot go out to experience the stories of the world, the world will come to share its stories with you. Through sharing, you have got a chance to change your world, change your mind, and to travel.

The *dervish* then shared a beautiful story with me: *Once, a travelling scholar came across a small drought-stricken village. On spending a day there, he realized the people were not meant to suffer such scarcity of water because, under the dry land, there once ran a river. When he told the people this, nobody believed him. So he started to dig, all by himself.*

Months passed, spading the earth. Everyone thought he was mad. But the scholar kept digging, and sure enough, deep from the belly of the earth, there came the first sound of water, as if there was another universe there, with water running swiftly. When people heard the beautiful sound, they rejoiced. It was indeed a moment of great jubilation for them. They helped him dig deeper, and together they built the first well in the village. It was a big well, mystical and magical. Soon, people started to draw water from it and were very happy.

One fine morning, before the world woke, the scholar left. Indeed, he was only a visitor, come to pay a visit to the water under the earth. And his work was done. So he left, leaving behind him the well, that wonderful source of pure water. Hundreds of people visited that well to listen to the story of the scholar. No one knew where he had gone or what else he was creating elsewhere. Eras went by but the well remained. Perhaps the scholar had ascended to another life, and taken birth again. But the well he dug remained, giving water to the people.

One fine day, another scholar walked into the same village. He saw that the people were struggling to draw water from the well. They were tired of doing this. What was the need for so much struggle, the scholar thought? He couldn't understand the hours people had to put in just to draw water for the day. So he came up with an idea for a duct that drew water up and out from a tap. The people could then simply open the tap and let the water pour out. When his job was done, before the sun poured out its million rays, he left the village. Why wouldn't he? He was a visitor. And a visitor's life, though short, has an immortal and invincible impact. A visitor is neither attached to the object nor is he fascinated with prolonging time. He is friends with time and lives by the nature of time. He comes and goes, and when he goes, what he creates becomes history.

Then after years, another scholar visited the village and saw the people settled in their lives. Their basic needs were fulfilled. He saw that the land around the village was fertile, and with the water available, cultivation was possible. He began to sow seeds and waited for Spring. When people saw the grain sprouting from the soil, they began to join him. Soon there were villagers farming and growing their own food. There was so much food that they could offer it to ten other neighbouring villages too. Then one day, before dawn, the scholar left the village, to find another temporary abode.

And then scholars were born in that land. They were learned. They knew how to dig wells, make taps and grow food. Soon, they became the 'visitors' visiting other lands, spreading their knowledge and wisdom.

It takes just one human to believe in his idea and to work on it, even if the whole world doubts. It takes only one visitor to enter into a life and change it forever, for generations to come. And it is beautiful to become such a visitor where life goes in a spiral from thereon. Growth never ends. Life never ends. It only expands. Your idea can inspire someone else.

The *dervish* looked into my eyes and asked, 'Do you know the meaning of your name, *Zaroon*?'

I still remember his trustful gaze. 'No,' I answered. 'I never thought of it.'

'Your name is the meaning and purpose of my life. It signifies that.'

'What is it?' I asked, curious.

'It means *Visitor*. Our life is about meeting these visitors and valuing them. Each visitor has a unique story to tell and a clue to the next journey,' the *dervish* concluded.

That night, before I fell asleep in the verandah, looking up at the bare sky, I told myself I would love to be such a visitor someday. I stopped struggling in my mind, thinking about Ahad and my different fates. Rather, I saw him as a visitor too, who had kindled deep reflection within me about my life. And that night, I chose my dream – to be a visitor here in this Home itself.'

Hearing this, Meru felt a sudden restlessness rise within her. She realized that she too, was a visitor to Zaitoon's house, and at some point she must return to her own home – her small, yet her own, abode in Bashirbagh.

$\mathcal{P}$

CHAPTER 52

Upon listening to Musa's tales about his journey with my *Abba*, Hyder, I was determined to know what happened after they went their separate ways. One could only guess what path *Abba* might have taken. Yes, the unforeseen situation had confronted him, just as the *Sufi* Master had warned. He certainly had to make a choice. From what I knew, he never returned to the *Sufi* Master. Nor did he ever go to Asmaar for initiation. What could have been the reason for such a turn? But whatever little information I could gather from Musa, made me love my *Abba* all the more.

So, here is what happened – a little innocent mystery.

One day, while they were on their way on the road to Mazha, where war had spread its reach and life was insecure and dreadful, they found a shelter located in a forest. It was the home of a woman with seven children. The woman was kind-hearted and loved her children. She and her husband had left their mansion in the city to protect themselves from the ravages of war, and took shelter in this wild wood. One night her husband passed away in his sleep and she was left alone to protect and raise the seven children.

While Mazha was a place that war seldom left untouched, the seven children grew up in the forest, surviving in a raw world. The woman wanted to cross the border to a neighbouring land, which was safe, to start a new life there. She was a learned and brave woman but she was afflicted with chronic bouts of anxiety. She was a city woman and loved people. In the forest she was isolated and helpless. She had seven futures in her hands.

That night, when Musa and *Abba* reached the forest and her abode, she generously cooked for them. She had learned to forage fruits, mushrooms, plants and edible leaves. While brewing some flowers for evening tea, she shared her story without making it sound like a sad ordeal. Then, before sleeping, she lit a candle outside her little hut and sat down to pray. She sat next to each child and chanted prayers with her jade *tasbih* in her hand.

The next morning, *Abba* asked her what her ritual meant. She told him that she was not the children's biological mother. They had lost their families in Mazha, and her husband had rescued them. When he had been alive, he would sit with this *tasbih* each night to pray, to connect the children with their ascended families, and to let their parents know the children were safe with foster parents. And he thanked *Allah* for blessing them with so many children.

At this point, Musa looked straight into my eyes and said, 'I certainly cannot tell you what journey your father, my beloved friend Hyder, took after I began my voyage back home to the palace in Pena. But I do still remember the name of the oldest boy the woman in Mazha took care of. It was Rashid.'

A deep silence filled me. I could feel incipient happiness building within me, a mote of memory waking up and simmering at the edges of my conscious mind. I could vaguely remember a forest, my mother's face, the dim lamp, the sound of crickets, the dense aroma of the wild woods, and little movements here and there. It was an unexpected revelation about my life. My heart welled up and tears fell from my eyes. I felt overwhelmed. Perhaps, I had found the treasure my father had spoken of. Our secrets are revealed in the most unexpected ways as if each has its own time to be unveiled. My father Hyder's destiny was not in being a *Sufi* apprentice, it was life itself.

I was an adopted child, one of the rescued ones. I was already a gift to someone's life. I felt so humbled by my *Ammi* and *Abba*'s gesture. I was taken care of. How big the heart of a human can be, and how beautifully a soul can be woven with love! I remembered *Abba* repeating the same prayer each night with all my siblings. Before we slept, we all sat in a circle, praying for all the worlds beyond our world, for all those beings seeking shelter and support, and thanking the warriors who fought so that we could live a peaceful and safe life. I remember my father sitting beside each of us with the jade *tasbih*, praying, until we were able to pray on our own for ourselves, and for the world.

○

Sitting by the lake I found I was a gift of love. Someone had prayed for me. I was grateful. Someone took care of me. I was grateful. Someone was happy I existed. And indeed, someone was always watching over me. From then on, I wanted to continue this ceremony of prayer each night, with my siblings. They were not my responsibility; they were my gifts.

I understood that the universe brought my *Abba* to Hasina, my *Ammi*, in the forest, and that he adopted us. My *Ammi* was a devout woman who passed away in her sleep after saying her prayers. I was very small at the time. She died as her husband had gone, peacefully. It is unbelievable how love begets love. Despite the grave circumstances, she believed that love was the only way and that her children, rescued with so much love, would be looked after.

'She may never have crossed the borders of Mazha, but she did cross over to the *light*. May the light always be on her pious soul,' Musa said. He stretched out his wrinkled hands from his ragged coat sleeves. 'Show me your palms,' he said gently.

I opened my palms, my fate lines still vague and incomplete. He gently placed something on my palm and closed my fingers over it. Then he cupped my palms in his. I still remember how fortunate I felt to be held by him. Whenever I feel depressed, I close my eyes and remember his palms holding my hands. Through him I can feel his love for my *Abba* and his respect for my, *Ammi,* and I feel safe. What else can children of this world want? To feel safe. To feel loved. To feel protected. To feel that they are seen and wanted.'

Musa looked at me and sighed. 'I have had this in my pocket for aeons now. It has made me feel safe, Rashid.' His eyes were tearful, his heart still missing my *Abba*. 'I have never shared this part of my life with anyone, but narrating our time together is not merely reminiscing about him from the vestige of my memory, but it ignites my spirit to still go on living my purpose.

Now, this is yours. Returning it to you is returning it to Hyder himself. What a humble Master he was, Rashid! You are so fortunate to be his son. He told me that one day I would know whom to give this to, as if he already knew. What a Master he was! May his mighty soul rest in peace. His *chilla* was in itself no less than an initiation. And he walked all his life as a *Sufi* Master. A silent one.'

Musa kissed my closed fist and let it go. When I opened it, there lay a large metal key.

PART VIII

CHAPTER 53

Musa's Tales

Bidding farewell to Hyder was not easy. How could it be? I was stupefied. But the old wise wax-seller's words adjured me to come to terms with the premonition of my return; that I was ready and it was time to return to my world – this palace. My journey back was not easy though. It was appalling in the beginning. There were times when I felt the urge to run away, but to where? And to whom? I had terrible hunger pangs when I found no food, and I wondered, how it was that with Hyder I had had the ability to stay without a morsel for days?

Without him, I felt the sun more harsh, the earth more barren, the nights more ominous, and the rains more menacing. I was put to the test. I was not following Hyder now, but my inner voice. I was buried in grief and found it difficult to keep the lessons I had learnt, alive. I had plenty of scars on my body. Unlike before, they took time to heal. It was ironic but I found myself getting more and more lost each day.

But I had many stories to tell people during the journey. I met many people along the way and continued to share insights. I became lost in those stories even as I narrated them. I saw myself in the men, the women, the children, in nature, differently. For the first time, I felt a compassionate heart beating inside me. I was a naïve man, a wise man, a visitor, a storyteller, a *fakir*. People called me by those names, even though I felt I was incomplete without Hyder and there was so much deeper seeking to be done. I would find myself repeating the words of Hyder to others. I sometimes spoke more for myself than for those who listened. You could say I had turned into a lunatic, a mad man.

Hyder once said, 'One cannot dig a well anywhere to find water under the earth. One first has to search for that land. And sometimes, this search can be a long journey in itself. When the well-digger finally finds that place, he puts his ear to the earth to hear the heartbeat of the water. Then he recites a prayer, picks up his spade, raises it to Heaven, and with all force and faith, hits the earth to crack it open. There, he knows his journey is now inward, inside, deep within, until he touches the heart of the water. That is how it is with us also. Finding a Master is a search, a journey. And once you find the Master, you know you can do nothing but dive in.'

The news of my journey and my stories reached many towns and villages, even before my arrival. I always wondered how that was possible. I certainly had stories to tell, because I had travelled far and wide. And by doing so, I found my purpose. *Stories!* Those human stories moved my life, starting with Hyder, and then in a never-ending stream of new tales each day. I consider myself fortunate, not only to have known Hyder, but to have walked with him too. It is such a gratifying feeling. Before I fell asleep each night under the vast open sky or under a white oak tree, I prayed to *Allah*, my heart overflowing with gratitude for the gift of Hyder. The thought of him comforted my burning heart.

Rashid, remember that travel brings experiences. It makes you fall in love. It helps you to know your purpose. It gives you the scent of freedom. And it beseeches you to do this often and *more*. We have all bid farewell to God to come live here on this planet and go on our own journeys.'

CHAPTER 54

Musa's Tales

One day, I woke to a deep pain in my heart, as if someone had thrust a sword into me. Despite the sign that I should return to my palace, something in me wasn't yet ready to take that road. It was then that this key Hyder gave me came to my rescue. He knew I would need it at some point. 'Take this, Musa,' he had said with a gentle smile on his face, placing it on my palm before we separated.

'But this is yours,' I said. 'This belongs to you.'

'It did indeed, once,' he said, composed, 'but now it belongs to you.'

There was no way I could refuse. So I honoured his wish. He kissed my palms. And in that moment I felt *Allah* touched my heart. The key became the most precious and remarkable memento for me.

When Hyder had visited my palace in Pena, I had presented him with a gift, as was the tradition in my father's kingdom, that an important guest should never leave the doors of the palace empty-handed. They were to be honoured with the best. And thus, despite knowing that Hyder was on his journey and was no less than a *fakir,* I insisted he accept a gift that was very dear to me, something that my *Ammi* had given me. He respectfully accepted and simply placed the key in his pocket.

There were times on our journey when I was so close to asking him to return the key, for it was my secret weapon, my only way to escape surreptitiously if needed. But that moment never came, until now, when the heavy sword pierced me deep within, hitting me with the realization that I will never meet Hyder again. Ever. I had lost him. Perhaps his physical presence wasn't needed, I thought. But no, it was! I was greedy. If not him physically, then his essence. Nothing I did could quell my thoughts of Hyder. If only I could meet him one last time! There was no balm for my ravaged heart.

Who knew that the key I thought I could use to escape from him was actually meant to escape to be with him? I started my journey with the gift, and when the time came, he quietly returned it. Though he never asked me which home, which door, the key fitted, maybe never even thought of it, for the period we were together, it belonged to him, and that which belonged to him could not be without his soul. It could not be without his spirit, his essence. This auxiliary thought gave me some solace. I yearned for a sliver of his soul, to help me gather the courage to go back to the palace, a place that had become unfamiliar territory for me. So, with my wounded heart bristling with love and loss, yet grieving the lack of both, I lived in a humble abode for days and nights and for many moons, in the remembrance of my Master, Hyder, in the city of Otto.

CHAPTER 55

Musa's Tales

My days in Otto had to end. I was as hesitant to step out of that home as a little baby afraid to come out of the womb, fearing separation from the mother.

It was an unusual day. The sun shone weakly amidst the lowering clouds in the sky. It had poured for days at length. I had set out for a walk in the woods when I met yet another old wise man. I was sitting under a tree enjoying the earthy fragrance of the wet earth when an old man appeared and began to walk around the tree in circles. His steps were slow. He would pause intermittently, look at the tree, open his arms, breathe, and then fold his arms again and bow to the tree. Then repeat the same actions. He seemed engrossed in his own thoughts, not aware of my existence.

Perhaps I should not have disturbed him, but I was curious, so I asked the man what his circumambulations were all about. He looked at me, unperturbed and put a hand on my shoulder. Then he looked up at the huge tree under which we both stood. I looked up too. It was a giant sequoia tree I believe, but I could not be sure. It was so tall that I felt I was standing on the edge of the earth and would fall off at any moment. I had never experienced that feeling before. The tree had many intertwined branches. The trunk had a spiralling structure and the leaves were of various shades of green. It was unusual to see a tree with so many different shades and shapes of leaves, and so many different shapes of branches!

'My friend,' he said in his slow husky voice, 'this tree is over a thousand years old. It comes from our ancestors.'

I looked at it again and my heart filled with feelings of abundance. Indeed, the tree had an ineffable, graceful and majestic presence.

'Have you ever come across something that has been living for a thousand years? Imagine the knowledge, the wisdom, the experience, the life, the stories that this being must contain. Imagine the number of flowers and leaves that must have come and gone; imagine the number of birds that must have chirped here and found their abode and built their nests and given birth to their little ones. Imagine the number of flies that must have waited for prey in its foliage. Imagine the number of people who must have walked by this tree or sat under its shade, to seek relief along their journeys. Imagine the weather that this tree has as memories within. Imagine the cosmos of this tree. Is it not enchanting?

And now, imagine the person who must have sowed the seed a thousand years ago. Imagine the heart and soul of the one who sowed something that stands immortal; something that is so gargantuan, alive and agile even after a thousand years. It is a privilege to see this tree in my lifetime. It is said that the one who sowed the seed was a bird rescuer. This man survived only on breath and sunlight, and rescued birds. One day, on his journey, he sat at this place where we stand today. May peace be on his soul! At the time, there was nothing here. It is said that when he was feeding the birds, he left some seeds and that is how this tree was born.'

I heard the old man, his hand still resting on my shoulder. He had gleaming eyes and a perpetual smile lit his face. 'But why were you going around this tree in circles?' I asked.

'See, this tree is born of both the seed and the soul. When I go around this tree, I feel protected. It carries the energy of a protector, where you feel safe.'

I listened to the old man attentively.

'There are people too, who are protectors. I feel that my purpose is also to be a protector, with whom people feel safe and loved. I have travelled for years to find this tree and it is giving me exactly what I need now – the strength to be a protector.'

In that moment, listening to the old man share his thoughts, all my apprehensions about going back to Pena vanished. I knew that it was the right thing to do. It was time to leave Otto.

○

My palace too, stood like a protector, waiting for its guardian. By the time I reached there, my father had ascended to another world, leaving this abundance as inheritance for me. Peace be on him. What our ancestors had built was now my responsibility. I was its guardian. So I opened it up for the people, for visitors, for travellers, for seekers, to come and rest for a while on their journey. Every day, thousands of people gaggle in to find food to eat, and shelter to rest, while some are here for the sights and some to paint the beautiful evening. Some cherish its shades and some its art. Some contribute towards the palace and some receive immense love and support from co-travellers.

The palace was a picturesque place, ablaze in the autumn sun. The lake possessed inner tranquillity, and the nights were adorned with constellations, celebrating the musings of the moon. Many artists found their inspiration here. Some write poetry, some whirl, some tell stories, and some surrender themselves in songs. This palace speaks to people in the language they understand as well as the silences of solitude. It brings answers to thirsty seekers and empty hearts.

And like any other guardian, I too, live outside the palace and witness the journeys of people unfold. They now call me a *dervish*.'

CHAPTER 56

Meru was ready. She packed her bags. She had been with Zaitoon for a year. And during that time she had travelled many miles within herself, and come to understand her own gifts of freedom and love. Unlike when she had arrived, she now had many bags to carry back with her to Bashirbagh. In this one year, she had not only accumulated a sea of knowledge but also *zari* work materials, new clothes, new shoes, some money, some books to help her study, and her notes on the life of Ibne-Al-Rashid.

Both friends had found great joy in teaching the children of the Home. They had narrated many meaningful conversations and stories from the book, and they had heard many in return. Some of the older ones now practised *zari* work on their own. Two of them were so gifted that they even joined Meru's team and worked on Gulfam *Kaka's* orders in an official capacity. And the library work slowly picked up pace. The news spread through the city and the Home received many gifts of books and writings.

The sun was about to set and the sky looked enchanting from the terrace. The creamy yellow sky stood distinctly at the horizon, the orange rays beaming all over. The red-tinged clouds hurried somewhere swiftly, and the birds huddled under the gables. A year had passed by like a roller coaster ride for Meru and Zaitoon. They had found a great treasure: *365 Days of a Sufi*. Now they knew what the *book*, the *tasbih* and the *attar* meant. They knew who the young royal prince in the wooden-carved frame that hung so grandly in the hall was. They now knew why Zaitoon's grandfather had asked that it not be taken down. They now knew who this home belonged to, who the Begum who bought the Children's Home was, and who her son was, who chose to become a *dervish* instead of a King.

Meru and Zaitoon's eyes had widened and their hearts raced as they tried to catch up with the revelations of this mystery one after the other. It was a jaw-dropping moment for them, their minds completely bewildered. Imperceptible truth! A gale-force silence had taken over their souls. What could they make of all that had been revealed? What they had discovered was an unimaginable notion. Yet it was true.

Now, seeing Meru ready with her bags, Zaitoon sank down on her knees; her stomach rumbled, her eyes filled with tears. She cupped her face in her palms and sobbed silently, her heart filled with love. Ambiguous feelings kept niggling her. She was happy to have discovered the truth of who she was, yet she was sad that her friend was leaving. In that moment, she missed her *Abba* to the depths of her soul. She wondered if she deserved so much love, so much abundance and inheritance.

'Tell me Meru, this is not a dream!' Zaitoon wept.

'This is your *niyamat*, Zaitoon. You have served your mother so well,' Meru replied gently. She sniffled, overwhelmed. 'This is your gift.'

'And yours too Meru, yours too!' Zaitoon took Meru's palms and kissed them gently.

Thereon, the house never felt the same for both the girls. They tended it with all their soul and love. It was a treasure that was meant to live forever. Not only did they feel overwhelmed by the secrets they had discovered, but responsible as protectors of the stories, and keeping them alive by sharing them with others.

As the two friends spent their last night together on the terrace under the star-spangled sky, having their peace time, swinging in gale and serenity, the Children's Home seemed coming to life; its numen now palpable.

'Our purpose was right in front of us Meru, but we had to take a long journey to come back here to find it!'

Meru nodded, her mind lost in the wonders of the past year.

'Does going back make you sad, Meru?' Zaitoon asked in a soft voice.

'A little but it is not bad. I now understand what Musa must have felt when he got the sign to return, leaving Hyder. But then, he wasn't alone. He was a wise man; he had his weapon of knowledge, sword of freedom, and sense of love in his heart. That took care of him till he returned to where he was meant to live his purpose.'

'You know Meru, you're talking just like my Grandpa!'

The two friends laughed jubilantly watching the city slowly slipping into the heart of the beautiful night.

'In a way Zaitoon, I too, am a visitor,' said Meru.

CHAPTER 57

365 Days of a Sufi

Month Twelve

One day, a *Sufi* was on a journey. He walked up to a mountain that nobody had ever been to before. There, he sat in meditation for days, and as he sat in this deep state, he experienced enlightenment. The whole world looked numinous. It made an indelible impression on him. It was an imperishable and enduring experience. In that moment, he lived his childhood, youth, adulthood and godhood. It was so blissful and tranquil that he wanted to share the wisdom with the world.

So he started to walk down and he realized that there was no pathway for people to come up this beautiful mountain. He thought how wonderful it would be to build a road so people could experience their own enlightenment, and then share the wisdom and power of enlightenment with others.

The *Sufi* came down to the town. Hearing of his experiences, the people of the town were ready to build the road up the mountain. They knew it would take a long time but they began under his guidance. Day and night they worked together. But, by the time they reached halfway up, the *Sufi* died, and no one knew what direction to build the road in. Nobody knew the path to enlightenment.

The night before he died, the *Sufi* had sat by a campfire and told them that enlightenment was not at the end of the road. That it could happen mid-way too, while on a pilgrimage. Also, enlightenment was not the end of the world or the end of seeking, but the beginning of understanding one's own purpose.

The next day, when he did not wake up, people were confused in which direction to go ahead with. Which way will lead to the right spot at the top of the mountain? There was no map. But one wise man among them suggested, 'Our job is to build a road, not to reach the right point. Hasn't this been our purpose?'

Together, in the name of the *Sufi*, they continued to work together to building the road. And one day, they finally made it to the top.

CHAPTER 58

Meru was happy to be back home. As she opened the familiar creaking door, her eyes fell on the patches of light on the floor. In the year she had been gone, the roof had cracked in places, letting in brilliant rays of light into the house. Meru scanned every nook and corner lovingly. The four walls, the floor, everything looked the same, just the way she had left it, other than the dust that had settled. Dust mites danced in the sunrays. The grimy windows held stains of muddy raindrops that had dried and cobwebs had indeed made their home in the corners.

Meru gently cleaned the muck off the cot and sat down on it. She looked at the picture of her parents on the wall, the corners of which had collected some grime too. Looking into their eyes her heart muttered, 'Thank you!' Tears flowed from her eyes. She missed them. Nostalgia enfolded her. She had come back to the same house, the same back-alleys, but she wasn't the same Meru. She was a transformed person.

She fetched her little *buksa* from the *almirah* and proudly placed in it the letters she had written to her *Ammi* and *Abu* while in Otto. They were her treasure.

From the door that stood ajar, she saw children playing, laughing and screaming as usual. Some were familiar faces, matured in a year, while others were new. Their voices made her feel at home. They had the same history as her. None of them had ever been to school, and most worked with their parents to help earn a livelihood for the family. Some simply lived on the roads. She remembered Esmail *bhai* and his pranks. It felt as if an era had gone by. Indeed, they had the same history but not the same story anymore.

She saw Rahim, sitting in a rickety wheelchair, watching the other children. He looked pale and frail, but his eyes shone bright as before, enjoying the children at play. Now and then one of them would come over to talk to him, including him in their jokes. How they had matured, Meru thought, sighing. Watching them, she knew what she had to do. She wanted not only to make the best use of her freedom but also to make it special.

That evening, the children gathered around her in her little room, to eat the sweetmeats she had brought from Otto, and to listen to her riveting stories. Sitting on the floor next to Rahim's wheelchair, Meru began living her purpose.

'Once upon a time, there was a starfish….'

$$\mathscr{L}$$

EPILOGUE

Month Thirteen

It was the thirteenth month and the three *Sufi* friends met in the holy place at the end of their long individual journeys. One had found *love*, another *freedom*, and the *third,* the path of *dreams*. As they sat around the campfire at midnight, they spoke of their travels and their encounters with the *Beloved*.

'And what now?' one of them asked when silence fell between them.

They looked at each other, wondering. *What do we do when that which we once longed for, that which we were seeking is no longer sought? It ceases to be a longing. What do we do now?*

As the three friends pondered on this wild state of their minds, the shadow of a bird passed over them at great speed, bringing a surreal breeze. They looked up and uttered together in surprise:

Huma!

They joined their hands and prayed, their hearts in ecstasy! They held hands and closed their eyes, thanking the *Beloved* for having bestowed *Huma* as the answer. And as they did so, *Huma* flew in closer circles and a beautiful golden halo appeared above them. They could not believe *Huma* had shown her face and was so close to Earth.

They heard the beautiful voice of the bird, melodious and gracious: *Fifty thousand years ago, I was here with my Beloved, at the end of my journey. It was the thirteenth month and my journey was over, not only in that life, but it was then my last life on Earth.*

As I sat across from my Beloved, pondering what to do with what I had received, he told me, 'So what happens at the end of the journey? You keep living, isn't it? When you have found your dreams, when you have found that love, and when you have found the freedom, you don't stop, you keep walking. You walk more. You do more. And you do more, anonymously, just for the joy of it, and this becomes your gift to the world. You gain knowledge, you share it. You have love – give it. You have freedom – use it. And this is the cycle that will always remain as human nature. And when you do this, you will live more – in the hearts of people.'

I heard the words of my Beloved. They were gems of wisdom. And thus, I chose the life of Huma. The one who is birthed in the sky and never comes down to the earth. People know me as a bird with special powers, but these are not any different from what you have inside you while you travelled, seeking. Such powers become special when you use them more, share them with others more, and continue to do so all your life, until you meet the Beloved again when you breathe your last. And all the special powers have wings that multiply as you live the alchemy of more.

The three *Sufi* friends heard *Huma* tell her story. She blessed them and disappeared into the darkness of the night sky.

Before dawn, the three friends commenced their paths once again, perhaps until another thirteen month – the month of *more*.

o

They might meet you someday on your own travels. And how would you know you have come across a mystic?

A mystic will never leave you without teaching you one special thing – the law of *reciprocity*.

And *Huma...* the reminder of *more!*

ACKNOWLEDGEMENTS

I have always wondered if we could perhaps title this page *Acknowledgements and Gratitude*. It feels more complete and in sync with the true reason this book came into existence.

First, I *bow to the Cosmic Force* that unites the human mind and universal intelligence. Thank you, Divine Force for giving us the opportunity to experience the world of imagination, intuition and feelings. Thank you Bio-energy and Nature, for keeping us alive and bringing our intentions into manifestation. Thank you all the Beings of Light up there! I acknowledge your visible and invisible presence.

So many people united serendipitously to bring this story into real expression. I want to thank the unknown artist whose art inspired me and opened a door to the characters that I did not know were waiting to be channelled. Thank you my first editor-friend, Nisha Joshi, who dove deep into the narrative with all her wit and creativity. Thank you my second editor-friend, Prabhath P, whose literary advice, and voice I truly respect and honour. I am so indebted for the time, energy, presence, and feedback of all my beta-readers, who opened their souls and became part of this work. We learned a lot from each other, and their vision and ideas helped me bring more life to the story and helped me crystallize my own imagination. You have special place in my life beta-readers: Zahra Shakir, Zaahira Gani, Akangsha Rawat, Shilpa M Menon, Sonia Uttamchandani, Amanda

Sodhi, Saumya Wafa, Nargish Sumrani and Sadik Keshwani. We now have a baby together. Congratulations!

How can I forget the one who called me to share the good news that the manuscript had been accepted: Rajeshwari Kejriwal. And my coordinator at Leadstart, Jayati Sarkar, who always shared a positive vision for the book despite the pandemic and lockdown. Thank you, Trupti Sawardekar, the Project Manager, and Kshitij Dhawale for the layouts. And my thanks to the designer Harshad Marathe for the lovely cover; the very face and feel of the story.

My thanks to my fantastic editor and guide, Chandralekha Maitra, who gave me insights and helped me navigate the maps and routes I had not considered walking within the story. Thank you for being patient with me, understanding my vision, and helping me stitch the world of words inside out.

And thank you Swarup Nanda, my publisher, who has always shared his space, and listened with respect about my work. I share the same respect for your dreams and aspirations.

My very life on this planet is because I am loved, accepted, and protected by my parents. I am nothing without them. My loving and generous mother, Yasmin Mackwani, and my loving happy-go-lucky father, Habibullah Mackwani, thank you for putting up with all my wildness in life. My gratitude also to my sisters and their families, my niece and nephew, and to our new family member – Olive, our sweet cat.

And to all the readers, seekers and breathers of the world; it is only amidst you that the characters' lifespan is enhanced and the story becomes immortal. So thank you for being out there, living in the invincible dimension called 'Reader'.

The characters of my book came together to teach me a particular virtue – to give *shukran* to and for everything. So, *Shukar alhamdulillah* to all of you, *Bismillah* to your new beginnings, and *Dua* for your journeys, until we meet again in the fields and meadows of other stories.

HEALING

is the gift we can give ourselves and those around us.

Everyone Can Heal combines three books in one:

Book I: *Healing Oneself*
~ The Connecting Process

Book II: *Healing Relationships*
~ You & I Are Beautiful

Book III: *Healing Loved Ones*
~ Being There

Every human being feels the need to HEAL at some point in life, and to find forgiveness, strength and understanding to live each day with positivity and grace. But what if the HEALER lies dormant within each one of us, just waiting to be invoked? Can the healer indeed become the healed? How uplifting to know the resources to heal both ourselves and those around us already exist – we only have to seek them within.

This unique book offers effective processes to heal the physical, emotional, mental, spiritual and other dimensions of human existence. Whether one is a beginner or an established healer, this book is a valuable guide to creating a life of consciousness and purpose. It serves as a basic handbook of living and a complimentary tool to other healing therapies one may already be practicing.

www.ingramcontent.com/pod-product-compliance
Lightning Source LLC
LaVergne TN
LVHW040003200726
843493LV00005B/1108